JUST ONE REASON

A WHAT HAPPENS IN  STORY

BROOKLYN SKYE

Entangled Publishing, LLC
2614 South Timberline Road
Suite 109
Fort Collins, CO 80525
Visit our website at www.entangledpublishing.com.

Lovestruck is an imprint of Entangled Publishing, LLC.

Edited by Alycia Tornetta
Cover design by Heather Howland
Cover art from iStock

Manufactured in the United States of America

First Edition August 2015

For April.
Not sure what I would do without you in my life.

Chapter One

Melody Sumner stared at the tablet's screen, letters and words scrambling like a dizzying carnival ride. *Not really moving, Mel. You know this. Just focus!* She glanced up to the circle of women around the table, blinked once, twice, and tried again to read the email.

Dear Karri, I am deeply confused by your intern's respon—

The tablet disappeared. Karri Wood, the well-known and highly coveted senior editor Melody interned for, cleared her throat, waving the device in front of her. *Well?* her blue eyes seemed to say.

Melody's hands fidgeted in her lap. "I…um…didn't finish reading it?" A question. Why had she made it sound like a question? Maybe it was the face-to-face contact she'd had with her mentor and publishing team the past few days during the Romance Lovers Convention, the meetings, workshops, and lunches that all involved discussing this year's releases and marketing strategies. The way these women stared at her when she was asked to read something quickly. Yeah, working remotely from home, where no one could witness *that* was much preferred.

Karri took a sip of her sangria and smiled stiffly. "Stop twiddling, for goodness' sake. I only meant to show you that when responding to agents and authors, you need to be clearer. We're interested. We're not. Give a reason and be done. Don't feel bad about rejecting their work. Lord knows we don't have time for that." She chuckled, her thick brown hair dancing with the movement, then patted Melody's shoulder. "And proofread before sending, dear. That way we won't have any problems." The punch to Karri's words elicited a bilious fizz in her stomach. Would this trip be it for her? The moment her mentor realized Melody wasn't cut out to be the successful editor she'd expected her to be?

"I'm sorry. I will," Melody said, then shoved her straw into her mouth and gulped her iced tea to keep from begging for mercy or making promises she couldn't keep, like saying mistakes as stupid as this one wouldn't ever happen again.

It's out of my control.

Across the table, Heather, the team's publicist, scrunched her nose at Melody, dipping her chin in an understanding nod, then barrel-rolled the women into conversation about the cover design on next month's lead title. Melody sighed and relaxed into her chair, silently thanking Heather with a smile. Becoming a romance editor was everything to Melody—a dream she'd had since she'd first discovered her mother's stacks of curled paperbacks years ago in high school. A guilty pleasure turned to passion, despite the difficulty she had with reading. Losing this internship would mean starting from square one, only with a black cloud of failure hanging over her head.

Melody tried to focus on the discussion at the table, but inside that niggling voice wouldn't leave her alone. The one that whispered she wasn't good enough, that her reading disability would keep her from following her dreams. College had been a melee of textbooks thrown across the room and ugly tears, and that insistent voice didn't want to let her forget it.

Melody sat up tall, planting her elbows on the linen-covered table, and shoved back her shoulders. *No. I can do this. I* will *do this.*

But could she? With errors like the email she sent to that agent?

Across the walkway, a hotel employee bent over a trash can and yanked out the bag, the collar of his red-and-purple uniform poking into his neck. Prickles built in her belly, the same as they always did when she thought of her father's words: *The Masquerade would suit you well.*

But she didn't want to live in Vegas, didn't want anything to do with hotel or casino life at all. She liked her quiet life in Southern California. Cute townhome, remote internship that would hopefully soon lead to a paycheck…that's what *suited* her. Just being at the Masquerade, with its Bourbon Street architecture and gaudy, jester-like decor, had her appetite disappearing faster than a magic act. Why had the convention been set here? Why not New York? Chicago? Plenty of locations would've provided a great venue for this rally of publishing folk —

A plate landed in front of her, the scent of tomatoes and

basil hitting her at the same time. "Your *basgetti* and meat-balls, ma'am," the waitress said teasingly. The women at the table laughed, and Melody grew warm in the cheeks. She hadn't meant to say that when ordering, but the rush to give her choice had tangled up her tongue.

She squinted up at the leathery face above her and forced a smile. "Thank you." At least everyone had thought it was a joke.

Story of your life, right, Mel?

Plates of lasagna, chicken parmesan, and a mound of garlic bread quickly filled the table. Melody lowered her hands beneath the table and shook them out—the hot burn of humiliation waning with the effort. Inhale. Exhale. *Okay, time to eat.*

From beneath the silverware, she tugged out the cloth napkin, accidentally sending the trio of eating utensils crashing to the tiled floor. Seriously? Did everything have to be a freaking fiasco with her?

Vegas… It had to be this despicable place throwing her senses—*and coordination!*—into a jumbled pile of doo-doo.

She pinched a thin smile, praying her cheeks weren't as red as they felt, when a man crouched down beside her to retrieve the silverware.

For a small second, she stared at the dark head of short-cropped hair beneath her. The square shoulders and the way they pressed against the sleeves of his T-shirt when he moved. *Please don't be one of the hundreds of cover models swarming this place.* After the day she'd had, she wasn't sure she could handle that kind of embarrassment in front of these women. The man's fingers swooped under the silver, and as he stood, his eyes met hers.

Forest green. A glint from the lighting above. Oh, those were not difficult to look into at all.

One side of his mouth pulled into a grin. "The filth on this floor probably causes cancer," he said, his voice lower than she expected and with a heavy—but not jumbled—Irish accent. "Better not use them." Quickly, he slipped behind her chair and snatched a new set of utensils from an empty table. Setting them in front of her, he added, "Enjoy your lunch," then crossed the walkway and entered Napoleon's, the hotel's renowned piano bar.

"Holy Colin Farrell," Heather whispered to the table. "That guy was dreamy!"

"Do you think he's a cover model?" Karri asked.

"Wouldn't doubt it. You know who he kind of looks like, though?"

Collectively, everyone—including Melody—shook their heads.

Heather tapped on her phone lightning fast, then held it up with a toothy grin, the screen displaying her favorite online magazine. "I should become a detective with how well I can recognize people. I was going to say he looks like Brendan Waterford, lead singer of Torn, this indie rock band in Ireland. But that's because *that guy* is his little brother, Declan Waterford. *The Pulse* mentioned him in an article about his brother a while back, said he'd had a few small gigs over in Ireland before coming to the States, but…" A line formed between her brows as she scanned the sign across the way that announced a dueling pianos show at nine o'clock. "You think he's performing here?"

She wasn't looking at Melody, but an answer came out anyway. "Yes," Melody said, swallowing against the wave of attention from the table. "My father's fiancée mentioned him not too long ago. Apparently, he can draw the crowds." Melody hadn't known who Declan Waterford was when her stepmother-to-be, Alexis, had talked of him. Didn't much care, either, since Vegas would only ever be a place for romance conventions and perhaps the occasional bachelorette party—*not* a permanent residence—so she hadn't paid considerable attention. *Irish charm*, she remembered Alexis saying. *Amazing arms, too.*

Well, Melody couldn't disagree with her there.

"I think our little intern made an impression on him," Karri said around the edge of her sangria glass. Discreetly, Melody grinned. Boss talking about men? Maybe a tad awkward.

Heather clapped her hands, spearing Melody with a smile. "Maybe he could be the one to finally lube your tubes!"

Lube my tubes?

"How do you..." Melody couldn't even say it, not in front of her boss. And how did Heather know about her Sahara-sized dry spell anyway?

"Oh, honey, it's written all over your face."

Declan Waterford peered once more over his shoulder at the gorgeous blonde sitting outside the Italian eatery. Not that he could see past those warm hazel eyes and the roundness of her tits in that fitted tank top—but both were pure flawlessness.

The door to Nap's shut behind him, and with it thoughts

of the girl, too. *Priorities, man. Savage as it is, you have no choice.*

Declan slipped a small radio from his bag, set it atop the piano, and lowered onto the bench. His fingers warmed up the keys in his routine series of chords before he switched on the radio and began to practice, matching the melody of the piano to the songs. He didn't care much about the lyrics— the audience loved when he ad-libbed those. But 90 percent of the songs he played in his shows were audience requests, so he had to stay up on all the American pop songs. And he prided himself on the little fact that he hadn't ever turned away a song for not knowing it.

Sam Smith turned to Rihanna to Katy Perry. Being some of the most-requested songs, he knew them already, but he played on, letting his mind drift as he did. Over the blonde outside, the strange rattle his car had made on the drive to work, and then to a conversation he'd had with his brother, Brendan. Not the last one. Just the one he'd forced himself never to forget.

What does this surgery involve, B?

Rerouting the nerves that no longer work to functioning nerves. It'll restore lost movement in my upper limbs. In spanner terms, brother, I'll be able to use my hands again. Need 'em to stroke the salami.

That was his big brother, forced into quadriplegia at the young age of twenty-six—his dreams stripped away with his ability to move all his limbs—and still making jokes about beating off. And to the very dickbrain who'd convinced him the water was deep enough. No doubt, had Declan been the one to jump first into the too-shallow water, he'd resent his brother fiercely. Blame him with every ounce he had in his body.

But that was the difference between him and his brother. Because if it had been the other way around, Brendan would've raised enough money by now.

The door behind the bar slammed, and Duey's voice echoed through the dimly lit lounge, over the sea of empty chairs. "Payday, bitch!"

Declan's fingers paused, drawing out the last note. "Pretty sure at my last job, my boss didn't call me 'bitch.' Is that legal here in the States?"

"If you work in Vegas, it is." Duey grinned, then slapped a white envelope in front of Declan. "Less than last month's because we had to deduct for last night's bar fight."

Less. Declan's mind stumbled over the word. "What?" he said, quieting the radio. "You can't charge me for that. I'm not the one who fought."

Duey scraped his hand over his pale face. "The fight you *caused*. Do I really have to explain this?"

"Did you see me once get off this bench?" *Less, less, less.* Growing antsy with nowhere to move, Declan stood, his insides exploding and crumbling at the same time. *Brendan doesn't have time for less!*

Duey stepped back as Declan marched past him. "Your words, bro. They get into people's heads, make them act" — he extended a finger to his temple and spun it in a circle — "like lunatics."

Hands clenched at Declan's sides. "My *lyrics* bring in good tips."

"With the ladies, yes. I've witnessed it, I know. But the dudes that come in here? They don't want to be threatened. By you or each other. Pit bulls, man. They're all just pit bulls in their own cages. Open one, and...well, you saw what happens."

Two grown men throwing themselves around the bar like idiots. Stools breaking. A few glasses, too. Yeah, he saw. Declan rolled his eyes. "Not my fault if 'roided-out tools come in here with beef already between them. Those guys probably spent all day at the pool, staring each other down. It would've happened wherever they landed."

Duey's mouth opened and closed, then he tucked his stringy black hair behind his ear—something he did when he was nervous, Declan had noticed. "Maybe," Duey said. "But insulting them?"

Like lightning, Declan's hands shot up, palms out. "Insults were never part of the show. I may kid, but I'm not stupid enough to risk my job."

"Neither am I, and after two episodes of this the boss now has his eye on me. Very closely. No more damage, you understand?"

Staring at the wall behind his supervisor's head, Declan nodded.

Duey pressed on, as if he knew he was pushing Declan's sanity button. "There are hundreds of performers waiting for this slot to open. One more screwup and you're out."

He hated the power trip this douche bag had over him, but he had to play it cool. Letting him dig under his nails like a splinter would only result in the guy receiving a face full of Declan's fist. Declan sucked in a slow breath, pictured his brother, and said, "There won't be another screwup."

"Good." Duey spun on his heels and started for the door. Declan knew this wasn't the time to ask but called out anyway.

"Hey, man, that opening at the Parrot Lounge? You think I have a shot at it?"

His supervisor didn't bother turning around as he spouted out over his shoulder, "Time, Waterford. It takes time to show you're deserving of that slot."

Yeah, and time is the only thing I don't have.

M elody scanned the table of chocolate-and-whipped-cream-smeared plates, her belly aching from the ungodly number of calories she'd just consumed. Dinner and dessert had passed with continuous—and exhausting—talk of her team's releases, an unending list it seemed would take them well into the following year.

She rubbed her head and caught Heather smiling at her. "I could use a stiffer drink," she said to the table.

Karri agreed with a nod. "And maybe some music?" Her eyes pointed to the door of Napoleon's, swung wide open now, with sounds of hit songs and laughter escaping. "Anyone up for a little break?"

Melody had to admit…she was spent. And a touch curious what that singing Irish accent sounded like up close. Quickly, she stood, smoothing the material of her skirt. "I'm in." She smiled. "And I heard Napoleon's makes a killer Manhattan."

The group of women sauntered into the lounge, beelining for the bar. The heaviness of the air, thick with heat and the stench of nicotine, had Melody rubbing her eyes instantaneously. *I don't know how Dad can call a place like this home.*

Drinks in hand, a few of the women headed straight for the dance floor. Melody hung back with Heather, watching as Declan Waterford skated his fingers over the piano keys. Graceful, yet steady. And assured. Almost as if the ivory was an extension of his own body. The man opposite him sifted through a handful of small white paper slips atop his piano. Song requests—what the entire show was based off. Salty-white strands of hair trickled down his sideburns and into a wild beard. Nice-looking, if you liked the *Duck Dynasty* look, but older and definitely not who she would have imagined onstage with an Irish performer. *Only in Vegas*, she thought with a giggle.

"You should request something," Heather said as the Vance Joy song came to an end. Melody tore her eyes away from the singer and stared at her coworker.

"I didn't come in here to flirt with the performers."

Heather cocked her head to the side, her braided ponytail draping over her bare arm. "You didn't?" she said playfully. "I thought for sure that's why you jumped up from the table so fast."

Her brain had felt scrambled from the three-hour dinner meeting, that's why she'd needed a break. But it wasn't like she could blurt that out to Heather—she didn't want anyone knowing, much less suspecting, that she struggled with all those words.

Another song started up, Declan's fingers racing over the keys. What had that study she'd recently read online said again about tying learning a musical instrument to the improvement in sound spelling? Dr. Mann, a well-known dyslexia specialist, often wrote about her theories on her blog, her latest relating to music.

Declan's fingers stiffened and jumped, the punch of sound vibrating in her chest. Seemed a bit far-fetched that learning to press a few notes could utilize both sides of the brain enough to *cure* her, but she had to be honest with herself. If someone back home had offered to teach her, she wouldn't have turned them down.

Poking her thoughts, the sound of Declan's voice drew her attention back to the stage.

Fingers off the piano, hand reaching for a glass of water, he looked down at the audience with a serious expression and said, "So my friend and I were walking down the Strip the other day and he'd a bag of doughnuts in his hand. He said to me, 'If you can guess how many doughnuts are in my bag, you can have them both.'"

The piano let out a *bu-dump*, the audience laughed, and then Declan glanced to the bearded man across from him.

"That song was fun, Randy, but we need something to get people out of their seats. That dance floor is looking as dried up as a nun's tit."

Someone gasped.

A few laughed.

Did he really just say that?

The other performer—Randy, completely unfazed by Declan's vulgarity—nodded and pushed a piece of paper to the side, then started into the tune of a familiar bar song.

"C'mon, people. Let's put some milk in this tit," Declan added, pointing to the open floor space in front of the stage. "Get up and get moving!"

At least half the audience crowded the dance floor, swaying, bobbing, jumping to the music. Any other time, "Don't Stop Believin'" would've had Melody dancing, too, but Declan's comment was still clinging to her. Was that really how the hotel wanted the show to run? Dueling piano performances were supposed to be classy, not offensive.

Doesn't matter, Mel, she scolded herself. *It's not like you work here.* Even so, her feet remained planted.

Declan's eyebrows danced as he sang, and women giggled from the dance floor below him like teenagers smitten over a member of a boy band. If he really was an up-and-coming star like Heather had said, she could see why. He had the looks, the voice, and obviously the ability to lure women in, but—

"Wow," Heather said above the noise, scratching her head. "I don't remember the lyrics being that...*rough*."

Melody nodded. "I was thinking that, too. Did he just say, 'Some were born to sing the fecking blues'? Is 'fecking' even a word?"

Heather giggled into her cocktail. "At least he didn't use the American version."

Across the dance floor, the sight of Karri talking to Taylor Blankenship, one of the romance industry's top-selling agents, caught Melody's attention. The two women mirrored each other with their arms folded over their middles, pinched brows, and faces tightening. *Uh-oh, they don't look happy.* Karri bobbed her chin and smiled tightly at Taylor, then scanned the room until her gaze landed on Melody. Speared her, just as Karri started her way. *Double uh-oh!*

"Yikes," Heather said over the song. "Did someone commit murder?"

"Looks like Karri might..." Melody answered, but in her head she was trying to recall if she'd ever corresponded with the agent on behalf of her mentor. She didn't think she had—couldn't remember, anyway, with the number of agents she emailed daily—and waited the eternity of a second that it took Karri to reach her, twisting and untwisting her hair.

An exaggerated sigh slipped from Karri's lips as she approached, cords twanging in her neck. "Don't get me wrong, I love coming to these events," she said, her tone harsher than usual and lips drawing into an uncommitted smile. "But I hate that people in the industry use it as a time to complain face-to-face."

Melody swallowed hard. "Complain?" *Hopefully not about me...*

Karri fingered the collar of her blouse, the other hand tightening around her cocktail glass. She gulped the fizzy liquid, then said, "A woman falling in love with a baboon, remember that manuscript?"

How could Melody forget? It was the most absurdly erotic piece of writing she'd ever read—definitely not apt for Karri's list, or their imprint in general—but Melody had to admit it'd been entertaining. So much so that she couldn't resist mentioning it to her Twitter friends. "I remember," Melody responded.

"Well, Taylor Blankenship is pissed because that was her client. And apparently my intern"—her stare focused directly on Melody's—"broke her nondisclosure agreement when she blabbed about it all over social media."

Silence. Even in a room blasting with music, Melody could hear her heart jump into her ears. Had her NDA stated no social media? Her insides sagged. She wouldn't know, because she'd spared herself the agony by not reading it. *And now you're going to be let go for it. Good going, blabbermouth.* Melody shook her head. "It wasn't...I mean,

I didn't — "

Karri held up her hand, her long cherry-red nails glistening in the murky lighting. "Spare me the excuses. I just need you to understand what being in this profession means. You are going to be in the spotlight, going to have writers who are desperate to have their work published hanging on your every word, so you need to be careful. The NDA is in place for a reason, and I need you to follow it to a T. Understand?"

Quickly, Melody nodded. "I understand. I'm sorry; it won't happen again." *And thank you, thank you, thank you for not firing me!*

"Well, then." Karri held up her glass. "Looks like I need another drink."

Melody released a bottomless sigh once her boss was on her way to the bar, swearing to herself she was going to read that agreement as soon as she got back to her room.

Beside her, Heather cleared her throat. "Cocktrough."

"What?" Melody snapped her gaze to her friend.

"You missed Mr. Irish say 'cocktrough,' as in the request jar was a cocktrough and he wanted us to jizz our best pecker snot into it." She laughed, crinkles branching out from her overly round eyes.

"Oh my God. Is he allowed to say things like that?" Automatically, Melody scanned the crowded room. Where was the manager of this place? Did he know what was going on in his bar?

Melody and Heather stayed planted at the edge of the dance floor as, song after song, the singer botched the lyrics with words like "ass juices" and "dingleberries." Irish curses, Melody assumed. And song after song, a strange yet irritated itch scratched at her belly. Not that she talked to her father much about the hotel—typically they avoided the subject, because hearing how her father dropped everything to come to Vegas and risked his entire life's savings to join the kitschy hotel business sent her stomach falling to her toes, just like that. She didn't understand how he could have been so reckless. So rash—with his money *and* his life. But watching this man onstage behave like an utter fool, when he was likely hired to do nothing but sing popular songs to an audience, had her blood growing warmer.

The song ended, and the bearded man said to Declan, "We've got an old-school request, D. You like Billy Idol?"

Declan shrugged. "A bit of a *neddy*. Which song?"

Randy passed an iPad over the pianos with a Cheshire-like grin, and after scanning the screen Declan belted out a laugh.

"Someone in here sure has fecking on the brain. Easy to do with so many beautiful women in here. All right, here we go. 'This is Dancing With Myself.'" Different from the other songs, Declan watched the tablet's screen—reading the music, Melody assumed—as he started to sing about no one else in sight on a crowded lonely night, waiting so long for a love vibration—

Suddenly, the music stopped. Declan looked at the audience. "*Love vibration?* What a lame phrase. Did you people really want me singing about a wanker pulling a skagdick?"

Melody's feet grew antsy. She felt like she needed to do something—anything—to stop this bad-mannered foreigner from offending people in the room. Setting her empty glass on a table, she said to Heather, "I'm going to request a song."

Her coworker bit her straw and winked. "Getting jealous of all the attention he's receiving from the ladies?"

Ha. "Something like that." Melody pushed through the crowd to the stage, where a stack of paper sat at the edge. Her mind raced for the perfect song—one he could in no way add profanity to, Irish or not. And then it hit her, and she nearly laughed out loud.

Quickly, she jotted down the name of the song, and just as she was about to drop it into the glass jar, a large hand swooped in and snatched the paper from her fingertips.

Oh, she hadn't noticed he'd stopped talking.

Then an Irish accent followed. "Guessing the songs women choose for me to sing is quite entertaining, you know?"

What will be entertaining is watching you sing it, you offensive yet ridiculously good-looking man. Melody tilted her head back and squared her shoulders, meeting his green gaze, fully aware that eyes all over the room were watching her. "Go ahead," she said, "but this one won't be so easy to guess."

The singer ran his tongue over his lips, a challenge in his eyes. Slowly he nodded and straightened. "Ladies and gentleman," he said boldly into the microphone, "I believe the missus here has dared me to guess her song choice."

Dared? Melody opened her mouth. "That's not—"

Words cut short with Declan's attention on her—his eyes brazenly taking in her every feature from head to toe. "Tanned skin, bleached hair...hundred bucks says she's a Cali girl."

A few *mmm-hmm*s behind her, and Melody bristled. *Lucky guess. Plenty of California residents come to Vegas.*

"What d'ya say, friends. Is her song of choice going to be from Kelly Clarkson or Lady Gaga?"

Shouts of both filled the room. Even Heather was in on it, hooting out "Kel-ly!" with a fist pump.

For a split second Melody felt like she was standing naked in front of everyone. Until, that was, she thought of the song title she'd written. Until she eased back and watched the dirty-mouthed Declan Waterford unfold the paper square. His eyes only widened the slightest bit—not even enough to notice had she been any farther away.

He didn't look at Melody, but at the audience, and shouted, "We're all wrong. Carrie Underwood!"

Randy clapped.

Heather clapped.

Everybody in the freaking room clapped.

Declan started to play a song that she hadn't requested.

What the heck just happened? No way was he going to swindle the room into thinking she'd chosen that song! He needed to pay, or learn his lesson, or…jeez, she didn't even know why she felt so determined to get through to him. Maybe it was the comment her father had made yesterday—*You've got executive blood, baby. We could be a great team.* His constant badgering to get her to live the hotel life. But picking up and leaving everything she had in California to manage a hotel wasn't what she wanted. Following her dreams into publishing was.

Still, she couldn't let this guy get away with ignoring her.

Swiftly, she reached for the first thing she could find— the leg of his pants—and tugged. "Hold on. What about my song?"

Declan's fingers kept playing, but he leaned down. "'Our God is an Awesome God'? No offense to the man above, but singing that would clear the room."

"So change it like you've been doing with the others," she challenged, narrowing her stare. *Then we'll see how much the people in here like you.*

He merely shook his head and blurted into the microphone, "Can't make chicken soup outta chicken shit. Ain't that right, friends?"

The audience laughed. Clapped. And fire erupted in Melody's chest. How dare he embarrass her in front of everyone? Her *boss*, who was laughing along with everyone else. The room suddenly felt like it was shrinking, pressing in on her.

"Listen, beautiful," Declan continued, eyeing the thin set of her mouth, "there's nothing in my contract that says I have to sing what's requested."

Melody had no idea if that was true. Still she gathered herself and managed a shrug. "I could have that changed."

Declan belted out a hearty laugh. "Yeah, you go ahead and schedule an appointment with the spanner who runs this stingy-ass place. If you're lucky, you won't be conned into working here, too."

Too? Was that what had happened to him? Did she even care? Arms folded, she lifted a brow. "Not very smart to say about your boss. *Or* the hotel you work in."

He leaned closer, the spicy scent of his cologne working its way to her nose. "Have you met him?"

The way he said it, disbelief and pure revulsion in his eyes, burned the tops of her ears. Her father wasn't a bad person—a businessman, yes, with a cutthroat drive to make the Masquerade one of the top hotels in Vegas—but he would never *con* someone into working here.

"Seeing as he's my *father*," she said, letting that last word hang in the air long enough to sink in, "yes, I have."

The music stopped. Declan's mouth opened, closed. She smiled.

He squinted down at her. "Michael Sumner—senior vice president of the Masquerade—is your father?"

Melody extended her hand, biting her cheek against a smile. That *oh, crap* look on his face was priceless, a nice revenge for what he'd done to her. But still not enough, so she wiggled her fingers and added with a punch in her tone so everyone in the room could hear, "Melody Sumner. I'll be sure to mention your name at breakfast *with Daddy* tomorrow."

Then she spun and headed for the exit.

Chapter Two

Shit, I just insulted the VP. To his daughter!

"Randy," Declan said, pushing away from the piano, "send us out on break."

"Not time, bro," Randy said, but he smiled and jerked his chin toward the door. It wasn't like he hadn't just seen what happened. Seen Declan throw away his job at the Masquerade before he could work his way to the top slot and earn enough money to fix Brendan.

Surely, Declan would be hearing about this after the show. Unless the boss man found him first. Or Duey.

Shit, he'd forgotten about Duey.

Declan sped up. He couldn't let that happen, couldn't lose this job. How long would it take him to find another? Unless…

The idea hit him as he stumbled into the main hall. Blinding white lights, the sounds of the casino in the distance—he shook his head, letting the thought settle into something that made sense.

If Melody Sumner had an in at the hotel…what if Declan used that to his advantage? Used *her* to get the most coveted show slot at the Parrot Lounge? Win her over, that's all he'd have to do. And how hard could that be?

Quickly, he searched the storefronts that lined the indoor footpath and spotted the blonde heading toward the lobby, room elevators just beyond. *Jackpot.*

Declan closed the distance with jogging steps, flinging himself into the elevator just before the doors slid shut with a *hiss*.

Only the two of them… *Well, at least I won't have an audience.* Melody flinched, probably realizing that, too. Then the elevator started to move, and a very silent and awkward five seconds followed. She looked at the doors. He looked at her. He was going to have to say something at some point— sooner rather than later, seeing as they only had a dozen more floors to travel. Instead he took that moment to soak her in. The waves of long hair down her back. The reflection of her face in the mirrored wall, revealing high cheekbones and full lips—more a product of natural beauty and not the gobs of makeup typical to Vegas girls.

"Listen…" he started to say, turning her way. Finger extended, she reached for the button to open the doors, but he swiftly blocked her hand and hit the stop elevator button. Her eyes grew wide, face paling. He threw his hands up to his chest, palms out to show he wasn't going to hurt her.

She scowled at him. "I don't want to listen to you," she said, a bitter sting to her voice. "I just want to go to my room and accept the fact that a performer humiliated me in front of an entire room of people. Including my boss."

Humiliated *her*? "Pretty sure it was the other way around, Cali girl. An attempt, anyway. You're lucky it was me who read that song request and not my partner. He looks friendly, but he's been doing this for a long time and doesn't take anyone's shit."

She shrugged noncommittally. "It won't matter by morning, anyhow. Not after I talk to my father." *And get your ass fired*, her squinty eyes seemed to taunt. She tilted her head to the side, shiny blond hair spilling over her bare shoulder. "A 'spanner,' isn't that what you called him?"

A sick feeling washed through Declan's core. If this girl talked to Michael Sumner, he'd be jobless by noon. And then what would he do? Look for another hotel gig? Sell himself on the street?

Okay, clearly he wouldn't go that far. But looking for a job took time, and…yeah, time was that thing that was definitely not on his damn side.

"Please don't tell your father."

She returned her eyes to his and folded her arms over her stomach. "You made me look like a fool in front of all those people."

He matched her stance, noticing how he towered over her, how she was the perfect size to pull her into his arms and tuck under his chin. *Jesus, Waterford, not now.* But how long had it been since he'd held a woman close to his body? Felt her warmth and softness? Her skin?

Months. Three, to be exact. It wasn't difficult to remember since the last hookup he'd had had also been the day he changed his brother's life. Bikinis and beers turned to a ride in an ambulance, a sterile hospital room, and a never-ending string of *I'm sorry*s.

He sighed and tempered his tone, bringing himself back to her accusation of making her look like a fool. "Which is exactly what you were trying to do to me when you requested that song."

"I wasn't trying to humiliate you," she snapped, shaking her head. "I was trying to get you to sing a song without adding in all those…those…*words*."

So that's what this was about? Was she kidding? "If people want to hear the song the way it's sung," he told her, "they can turn on their bloody radio. Those *words*—those *jokes*—are what bring in the tips."

"It's degrading."

"It's *Vegas*." A beat of silence, and a smile started creeping up his mouth. Couldn't argue with that reasoning.

A few steps in reverse and she pressed up against the back wall. Her round ass touching the metal bar like that… For a split second, he might've wanted to be that bar, wanted to touch her there. But then she opened her mouth. "And it's not what my father wants in his hotel." A strange expression came over her face just then—an odd mixture of confusion and something else, as if the words tasted bad and she was trying to spit them out. It was there, and then it was gone, like a glitch on a screen. Quick enough that it made him doubt he'd seen it at all.

"You can't tell him." Declan's feet itched to move forward, to get up in her face and explain exactly why—to tell her about Brendan. She'd understand, right? Instead, his mouth spit out something else entirely. "I've been trying to move to the night slot at the Parrot Lounge. I'm already on probation with my supervisor. If he or any of the bosses find out I haven't been following policy, I'll never get promoted."

"And that's my problem how?"

"Because I could use your help. Put in a good word for me, maybe?"

A laugh flew out of her mouth. A quick, short *ha!* "You want *me* to put in a good word for *you*?"

"Please." Damn, this was not working. "I'll do anything."

"Anything?" Melody's hands rested on the metal bar, steadying her. Being this close to him, his body so… big, was unnerving. And Heather's mention of Colin Farrell wouldn't leave her mind. The voice—even his clean-cut look—screamed stageworthy. And he was a musician. Despite the jerk he had been, this could be the perfect trade. She squared her shoulders. "Can you teach me to play the piano?"

A wrinkle formed along his brow. "I assumed you were from out of town."

"I am. California." She smiled and then kicked herself because it was way too easy to smile at that attractive face. "Guess I should've said, 'Can you teach me to play piano in the next few days?' I'm here through Sunday."

"You want to learn to play the piano in a few *days*? I'm not sure that's even possible."

It had to be. Mistakes were happening more and more. And Karri, she could tell, was beginning to grow less patient with them. If Melody kept messing up, it was only a matter of time before her boss grew tired of cleaning up her messes. "Please."

He glanced at her, and his eyes felt like fingertips, sliding over every inch of her face. "Why?"

Because I was born with a processing deficiency. Because the focus it takes to play an instrument is supposed to help untangle the knots in my brain, and let's be honest here, there are lots of those knots, and I'm desperate to unravel them. She tried to keep a straight face, not let the warmth in her chest creep into her cheeks, and managed a shrug. "Childhood dream, I guess."

"That you're now fulfilling at the age of…?"

"Twenty-three." She gripped the bar harder, hoping he wouldn't hear the bobble in her voice. "And, yes, I'm just acting on it. Is it a deal or not?"

Silence echoed throughout the tiny elevator, just a beat before Declan nodded. "We have a deal. Meet me at Nap's tomorrow, noon."

B utterflies. Why did she have butterflies? It wasn't like Melody *liked* Declan Waterford, but as she tugged open the heavy wooden door to Napoleon's, she couldn't seem to convince her stomach and that fluttery feeling otherwise.

Bright lights glowed in the room, a bleached sheen over an alcohol-sticky bar. Chairs sat upside down on the tables, better revealing the gummy spills from last night's customers. Obviously, the place hadn't been cleaned. But why?

Stingy-ass. Declan's comment from last night burnished under her skin. Was her father skimping on help for the hotel?

"Don't mind the mess," someone from behind her answered. Declan, she knew immediately, expelling a quick, relinquishing breath. *I might not like Declan Waterford, but I can't say the same for his accent.* "Cleaning crew is running late. Good news is that we have the place to ourselves. Bad news, however, is you'll have the rancid stench of day-old alcohol in your nose long after you leave."

Melody spun on the toes of her wedges, a rogue smile tugging at her lips. The thought of learning to play an instrument—of testing out Dr. Mann's theory and possibly killing off the threat of losing her internship—had her grinning wide for the first time since she'd walked away from Declan and his desperate plea to keep her mouth shut in front of her father. "You say that like you've done this before."

Hands in the pockets of his black shorts, he approached her, shaking his head. "Didn't have a piano when I first moved to the States. Had to practice at work. Still do when my roommate works the night shift." She watched his mouth as he spoke, the way the strength in his bone structure contradicted the soft, inviting appeal of his lips.

Wait. Lips? Why was she looking at his lips? *Noticing* his lips?

Think of something that doesn't have to do with his lips!

She looked at the ceiling, scrambling. So he had a roommate. Hmm. She hadn't expected that.

"Should we get started?" He gestured to the piano onstage; at the same time she inhaled a shallow breath and tried to drown out the smooth sound of his voice as it slipped into her ears and infiltrated every cell in her body, heating her in places she had forgotten existed. But the person that sexy voice belonged to was also the one who'd sat at that piano last night and made her out to be a California cliché in front of a roomful of people, including her boss. The sight of it burst something hot and cutting into her that warred with the peculiar pull his voice had on her. She swallowed. She nodded. Then she started for the stage. Sure, he might have humiliated her, but getting free lessons was her retribution.

And hopefully her saving grace. According to Dr. Mann, many patients had already claimed seeing a difference in their reading and writing. She'd wanted to find a music studio in her hometown, but with her internship taking so much time, she'd barely had a chance to look. Timing, she had to admit, was perfect. Regardless of the slight fib she'd had to tell her boss when she was asked to join the team for lunch. Feigning a lunch date with her dad was well worth the possibility of stimulating her brain to improve her literacy.

With careful steps, Melody followed Declan up the side stairs and onto the wooden stage. In the center, two black pianos faced each other, one already uncovered. The butterflies scrambled in her belly. She had never touched a piano in her life. *Am I going to make a complete fool of myself? What if I can't get the rhythm? Or hear the notes the same as he does?*

Maybe this wasn't such a good idea.

"I've never taught someone to play before," Declan said as he slid out the bench for her to sit. "I guess maybe we'll start with some chords and go from there?"

She lowered onto the cushioned bench, resting her hands in her lap. "Um…" She cleared her throat and said, "I have no idea what a chord is. You're going to have to start more elementary than that."

He sat beside her, his leg and arm brushing hers within the small space, sending a wave of chills crawling over her body like a colony of ants. *Oh, dear…* He pointed to a white key in the center. "How about middle C? Have you heard of that?"

Well, this was a tad more embarrassing than she'd expected it to be. She shook her head with a shaky giggle. "Other than listening to the radio, I've never really been around music."

Unexpectedly, he lifted her right hand from her lap, extended her index finger, and placed it on the cool white key. "All right, then. Melody— Wait." He tilted his head. "What's your middle name?"

She smiled. This was a little weird. "Marie," she answered anyway.

He matched her smile, only to her his felt so much brighter. Like this whole thing wasn't uncomfortable and awkward and unsettling for him at all. "Melody Marie Sumner," he said, "meet middle C." Firmly, he pressed his finger over hers, filling the room with a strong eruption of a note. Warmth spread down her fingers and into her wrist. Was he trying to get her to blush?

"I take it there are other Cs too, then?"

"Yes, but we'll get to that." He spent the next few minutes introducing Melody to each of the notes in the center of the piano. Once she could name them, he demonstrated a scale, deftly gliding his fingers one by one over the stretch of the keys.

Melody attempted to copy his movement, though her fingers tripped and tangled with each other. "You make it look so easy," she said, shifting on the seat to put a sliver of space between them. Sitting this close—with his intense gaze and face so smooth she wanted to run her fingers over the flawless skin—was messing with her head. Jumbling her thoughts.

She wasn't attracted to Declan. No…it had just been so long since she'd been this close to a man. *Yeah, you keep telling yourself that, Mel.*

Not that it would matter, anyway. She lived over three hundred miles from Vegas, from him, which meant nothing could ever come out of being attracted to him.

Ha, so you are attracted to him! First step is admission, right? She ground her teeth. Her brain really needed to stop thinking.

"First of all, you need to loosen your fingers a little," he said, taking her hand in his. Slowly and with precision, he guided each of her fingers to the right keys, tucking her thumb under to finish out the scale. From the corner of her eye, she couldn't help but notice the way his T-shirt stretched over his biceps with the movement—the lines of muscles beneath the thin material. It was…it was…distracting.

Gah, she seriously needed to focus. This wasn't about the sudden gooeyness she felt pooling in her stomach. Or was it? Could it be?

Oh, dear Lord. Apparently sitting leg to leg with someone of the opposite sex had her thinking like a crazy person. *He isn't interested in you, anyway. Remember, this was a deal. To save him from losing his job.*

Still, it took everything in her to concentrate on gliding her fingers up and down the keys the way he'd shown her. And though the rhythm wasn't as smooth as his, she eventually mastered the skill. Next were the chords—a series of three keys she played in unison—which wasn't so difficult once she managed to find the correct placement of her fingers.

"So what brought you to Vegas?" Melody asked Declan

as he was stretching her fingers over the next sequence of keys. *D chord*, she reminded herself. After thirty minutes of his hands manipulating hers, the feel of his skin on hers was no longer foreign. The softness of his fingertips, the gentle way he moved her about... It was as if he'd been touching her for years. And that's how she felt him stiffen with her question. Though he didn't stop with the location of her fingers, there was a definite pause. A flinch.

She'd done her research last night—Googled his name and read the article Heather had mentioned in *The Pulse* about Declan's brother's band and how Declan had started out as a tagalong to Torn before taking on some small gigs himself. Not much about his personal life, however, so with that slight recoil, she was suddenly intrigued.

"Vegas?" No way was Declan about to explain what brought him here, especially after the ass he had been last night, calling her father out as a penny-pincher to her face. Stealing his brother's freedom and music and... well, *life* wouldn't at all help him redeem himself enough for her to not want to run and tell her father that hiring him had been a mistake. No, he had to play nice. Nicer than nice. "Who doesn't love Vegas?" he answered casually with a shrug, at the same time correcting the angle at which she held her fingers.

She tilted her chin toward him, her hazel eyes skimming over his face. Eyes the color of the changing of leaves in the fall. The perfect blend of green and brown that swirled together, revealing everything and nothing all at once. Behind her questioning gaze, something darker lurked, though. Hardly noticeable, but definitely there.

What were her demons?

What drove her to demand a few days' worth of music lessons from a total stranger? He knew learning to play wasn't a childhood dream she was randomly acting upon. People just didn't do that. So why was she here?

And why was she so curious?

He lifted a brow, turning his head to meet her gaze straight on. "What about you? What brings you to Vegas?" Even as the minutes passed and she grew noticeably more comfortable around him, he couldn't stop imagining running his fingers through that silky hair. Over those red-stained lips.

"The Romance Lovers Convention. I'm an editorial intern, and the editor who mentors me asked if I would come. She wanted me to attend some of the workshops the conference is offering." The darkness in her eyes flared.

And so did Declan's interest. Declan cocked his head, unable to take his eyes off her. "And you're learning to play piano to impress this mentor?"

Melody focused on her hands. "I guess you could say that." Then she cleared her throat. "So your brother was in a band?"

"Somebody's been stalking me," he said with a smirk.

"Not stalking. Just ensuring my safety won't be in question when I'm alone with you."

"I didn't leave Ireland with a police record, if that's what you were wondering. Except for that one time I was caught bungee jumping off a bridge. Apparently, you can't jump off just any bridge."

Melody narrowed her eyes and assessed him. "I thought everyone knew that."

He smiled. "Yeah, that's what the cops said, too."

"You're into extreme sports."

He shook his head. "Guess you can say I went through a reckless phase. But"—but losing his brother put the kibosh on that real quick—"I'm much more mature now," he said instead.

"So you left Ireland because…"

"I guess you could say," he said, his words coming out much too harsh, like they always did when he thought about the last few months he'd spent back home, "the indie rock scene over there just wasn't my thing." Not after the accident, anyway. Too many reminders of his brother. Too many opportunities to let the guilt dig into his chest. He hated that it did, and he hated that everywhere he'd gone questions about his brother followed.

He could tell by the way Melody's eyes bored into his that she had more questions—likely about how he'd landed here at her father's hotel—but the roughness of his tone cut them short. In that moment, he felt something in him crack. Barely there, but enough to regret roughening up his voice for her.

An ass again for taking his mistake out on her.

Gently, he slid his fingers up her wrist, straightening the position of her hand. "I didn't mean to snap."

"It's all right. I shouldn't have pried into your personal life." With that her gaze skittered down to his mouth, igniting a hot flash down below his belt. Did she want to kiss him? Even after she'd acted so turned off with him last night?

The mystery of it magnified the question tenfold. What

would she feel like? Taste like?

He only allowed himself those two questions before slamming the thought away. *Brendan first. Brendan first. Brendan first.*

"Close your eyes," he told her, wrapping his fingers softly around her slim wrists. She eyed him warily, so he added with a teasing grin, "Don't worry. I'm not going to kiss you."

A light laugh sighed out of her lips, and then she lowered her lids. He tried not to notice how beautiful she was now that he had a chance to really look at her. How her high cheekbones bled into a perfectly shaped button nose. How her lips weren't quite even—the bottom slightly fuller than the top—and rested with a splinter of space between them.

Tried.

But failed.

"I want you to listen to the sounds this time," he said, still watching her face. "We're going to play a song."

With a scrunched-up nose, she snorted. "I can barely play notes in order. What makes you think I'll be able to make any sort of music?"

"You doubt yourself so easily." Carefully, he took her hands and arranged them over a low-end E minor chord, then an A minor, then G. Slowly, her lips twisted up into a smile.

"Hey, I know that song. It's one of my favorites."

So he'd pinned her right—the type to like that soulful kind of rock. Hozier was one of his favorites, too.

"The rawness of it," she continued, opening her eyes, "is so powerful." For a small moment, she nibbled on her bottom lip. If she was his, he would tell her not to do that because her smile was too beautiful to damage. But strangers didn't say that to each other. Besides…she would never be his, no matter how sitting next to her made him feel, because by the time he earned enough money for Brendan's surgery, she'd be long gone, back to wherever it was she came from. "You sang it last night," she continued softly. "It was the only song you didn't change the words to." It wasn't a question, though the lift in her voice gave it away that she was asking.

He shrugged. "A song about worshipping a woman's body? I wouldn't change that for anything." Quickly, he looked away. Why had he said that to her? And while his hands were cradled over hers?

When he brought his eyes back to hers, she hadn't moved. Her lips still rested a sliver apart, only now glimmering with recent moisture of her tongue. "You think that song is about a man worshipping a woman's body?" A line dipped between her brows as they puckered together. "Who is the church, then?"

Talking lyrics—deciphering them—was something he'd always done with his brother, ever since they were out of grade school. It was entertaining and challenging and…oddly erotic doing it with someone as striking as the woman sitting beside him. He let that thought go and explained, much like he would've if he'd been with his brother, "Two people, not just fucking, but making love so passionately…that single moment when a man gives himself over to a woman, when he is her…church. Only a dumbass would screw with the brilliance of that song."

The backs of his fingers slowly traced the length of her arms, and a tiny gasp whistled through her teeth. His hand stilled. Fuck, what was he doing? And why did the tingle in his fingers feel like a surge of satisfaction? Why couldn't he pry his hand off her?

Goddammit, Waterford.

Beneath his touch, she shivered, and he couldn't help the images that shot through his mind — his hands, his mouth ravaging and worshipping her until their bodies glistened with sweat.

Fuck!

No. She was just a tool to get enough money to fix Brendan. He. Could. Not. Hook. Up. With. Her.

"I never thought of it that way," she suddenly said in a breathy whisper, rigidly stiff yet melting under his touch at the same time. God, she was sexy when she was relaxed.

Just one kiss, his mind threw at him. Hard and fast and unexpected enough that he had no time to block it. *Just to see what she tastes like.*

If he kissed her once, maybe he'd be able to expel the thought from his brain. Be able to continue this lesson without his eyes glued to her mouth and his mind circling the idea. If he kissed her once, just once, it wouldn't do anything to get in the way of what he was trying to do for Brendan.

If he kissed her once, he'd walk away and never think about it again.

Gliding his fingers up her arm then her shoulder, he hooked his finger beneath her chin and twisted her face in his direction. Damn, she smelled good, like his very own peach cobbler. "I really want to kiss you," he said, running his thumb over those uneven lips.

She gasped.

Then she licked her lips.

And that was all the confirmation he needed to cover her mouth with his. Warm, citrus-flavored lips pressed gently into his, and her hand immediately found his shoulder, as if she needed to grab onto something in order to steady herself. His hand slowly trailed all the way up her back until he was touching the stretch of skin just below her hair. He tightened his grip on her neck, and then he parted her lips with his tongue, sweeping in for a taste.

A fucking glorious taste.

She tilted her head so he could taste more of it. Her hands no longer had hold of his shirt. They skimmed his neck, shoulders, chest as she leaned into him, pushing her tongue deeper into his mouth.

He slid his hands back down her spine until he reached the round curve of her ass, gripped it hard and brought her flush against him, needing to feel her softness pressed into him, even if only for this once. God, she fit perfectly.

She broke their kiss, easing back, a strange look on her face. She wanted this. But didn't know how or why—

"I'm sorry, Melody. I didn't mean to do that."

"Don't apologize," she said in a rush, still breathing hard. "I wanted to. I just…" She reached up and touched her lips, a stain of pink growing on her cheeks. "I just don't do things like that."

He smiled. *At least we're on the same damn page for that.* "I don't, either," was all he said.

Slowly she nodded, her fingers gently skimming the muscles of his abs, and then she had his shirt pushed up to his chest and he didn't even know how that had happened. He was okay with it, though—*very* okay. With the tip of her fingernail, she traced the lines of his muscles until her hands dipped just inside his jeans, against his skin, and a surge of lust—hot and hard—jammed into his brain and overpowered any logical thought he was capable of having.

With her legs positioned against his sides, she straddled him. Without thinking, his hands shot up her back, searching, searching for skin to connect with. They found it at the nape of her neck, warm and soft, and clung to it while she devoured his mouth again. Tasting him, filling him.

The sound of the door swishing open then closed echoed around the name he heard called into the room.

His name.

In the pissed-off voice of his boss.

Shit.

"Oh my gosh," Melody said, jumping up from his lap as he tried to steady her and pull down his shirt at the same time. It took a few seconds—Melody's eyes wide and looking very much like a teenager caught by her father—until Declan had the nerve, and if he had to be honest…his breath back, to face his supervisor.

Duey scowled. "Really, Waterford?"

"It's not what it looks like," he said in a rush, his hands up by his chest, palms out. Damn, had his jeans shrunk a full size? Running his fingers through his hair, he stood, placing himself between Melody and his wound-up boss. "I was giving her piano lessons."

Duey belted out a laugh. "You're shitting me if you actually think I'm going to believe that."

Declan's mouth open then closed. Duey was right. He was so screwed. "Listen, Duey—"

His boss held up his hand. "No, you listen to me, you little prick. This is my bar, and I'm tired of your constant disregard for it. Do I have to spell it out for you like a child? Bar does not equal a place for your personal pleasure." He pointed to the uncovered piano. "This belongs to the hotel, which means you can't do whatever—or *who*ever—you want on it. What would the boss man say if he walked in and saw *that*?"

A weak clearing of a throat resonated from behind him. Duey and Declan both turned to stare at the blonde standing at the edge of the piano. Her silky-smooth waves fell over her shoulders, hands clasped in front of her. And those uneven lips, swollen and red from that kiss. An upwelling of pride filled Declan's chest. He'd done that.

"I'll tell you what he would say," Melody said, visibly swallowing against the shakiness in her voice. She looked at Duey, then to the grimy floor and sticky bar. "He would wonder why the manager is incapable of getting his cleaning crew here on time. And why that manager was also calling his employees 'little pricks.'"

Duey rolled his eyes and pointed to the door. "Take your shit, Waterford, and don't come back tonight. I'll get Riley to fill in."

Fucking Riley Banks. The one performer who'd been itching to slither into Declan's spot at Nap's. "You're replacing me with Riley?" His insides burst with fire and froze over with ice at the same time. "What the hell?"

"No." Melody stepped forward, hands now at her sides, shoulders back. "I insist you let Declan do the show tonight."

Duey's harsh laugh filled the room. "You, Miss Do Me on a Piano So I Can Go Home and Tell All My Friends I Fucked a Vegas Performer, insist?" He threw his arms out wide. "Negative."

Declan cringed at the name, but Melody only took a step toward him, eyes on his boss. "Whether or not I wanted to *do* this man is none of your business. But you will let him perform tonight, unless you'd rather hear it from Mr. Sumner himself." Duey squinted his dark eyes at her, surely calling her bluff. *Ha, just wait.* Melody tilted her head to the side, a cute little crinkle forming between her brows. "Daddy and I are meeting here for drinks tonight."

Eyes wide, mouth closed. *Is that what I looked like, too?*

Duey eased a step back. "*You're* the daughter he wants to turn the hotel over to?"

She smiled, though something about the way her lips drew upward felt forced. Was she lying about dinner just to make Duey squirm? And what did he mean by "turn the hotel over to"? Attention on Declan, she said, "You already know my song request." And then she strutted off the stage and out the door.

Chapter Three

Turn the hotel over to? Had Melody heard that man wrong?

No, that's what he'd said. But…her father had only mentioned managing the hotel. Not taking it over. Completely? Was that what he'd meant? And if so, why hadn't her father said anything?

The thoughts wouldn't leave her alone, even after she had gone back to the Romance Lovers Convention. Sitting beside Heather and Karri, listening to speaker after speaker discuss drafting blurbs and marketing strategies, all she'd thought about was why her father was suddenly willing to turn the hotel over to someone else.

Was he sick? Dying? Going to pick up and move somewhere else? Ugh, the race her mind was running was too exhausting.

Back in her room with the meetings done for the day, she exchanged her brown skirt and blouse for something more comfortable—cutoff jean shorts and a flowy off-the-shoulder top. The peach one, her favorite. She threw on her white Chucks, feeling much more at ease in her normal clothes, and headed downstairs.

Jangly music and the whir of spinning reels filled the huge casino as she made her way to Napoleon's. The Masquerade Hotel was grander and more ostentatious than most others on the Strip. Larger even than the Bellagio, but much less tasteful, with its disquieting expanse of colorful beads and ribbons draped over every exposed surface.

With a few minutes to spare, she wove in and out of the slot machines, watching as the majority of them hit near misses. It was the preprogramming, she remembered her father telling her. *A near miss makes players feel as if they almost won a huge jackpot. That if they play some more, they will win.*

Conning people into giving their money to the hotel. Yeah, it just wasn't something she had any interest in. She wanted to edit stories that would touch people. Help people. Give them a place to escape to. Make lives better with words. Not for the money. No, she was actually quite comfortable in her simple townhouse in the suburbs outside L.A.

Strolling down the hall toward Napoleon's, her eyes skimmed the signs, posters, anything that had words—a habit she'd had since a child. Alongside it came one wish—to one day look at those words and not see a scrambled mess of letters. *Maybe after a few more lessons with Declan...*

Every part of her body flushed hot at that thought. What had she been thinking? Jumping his bones in the middle of a hotel lounge? Her *father's* lounge?

That was the problem, though: she hadn't been thinking.

One hundred percent *not thinking.* Who did things like that? Made out with a complete stranger just because his touch gave her chills and his throaty voice, whispering words about passion between a man and a woman, flushed through her body? She'd been consumed.

She'd been an idiot.

So why couldn't she stop thinking about that kiss?

The way his lips could sing *and* drive her to straddle him like a sex-crazed madwoman. What would've happened if his boss hadn't walked in? Would she have ended up naked on the piano, *Pretty Woman* style?

She laughed to herself. Not a chance. She had more control than that. Besides, it wasn't like Declan Waterford actually liked her. She knew full well that he was using her to get a promotion with her father just as much as she was using him for lessons. What they'd shared today was a business deal. An exchange, a last straw for her not to lose this internship for a good word to her father. That was it.

The entrance to Napoleon's lit up with the golden glow of lights, the doorway already crowding with young, miniskirt-clad girls wearing far too much makeup. Cute, though—the type someone like Declan Waterford might go for.

Did that bother her? Was that why there was a slice of irritation in her chest? Or was that because her father hadn't told her his intentions?

As she shuffled into the room, she inhaled a bottomless breath and put on a smile. Forget those girls, forget Declan Waterford. The next hour needed to be focused on her father and convincing him that she would never, ever be the one to manage this hotel.

Sitting in the back of the room but dead center from the

stage, where two unoccupied pianos sat, her father spotted her and waved. An empty tumbler sat before him, and Melody sighed. Not that her father had a drinking problem, but since his divorce from her mom and relocation to Sin City, his ability to down a highball of whiskey had outweighed the control he had over his mouth after.

"Hi, Dad," she said carefully, lowering into the chair across from him. The dim lighting in the room darkened his already gray hair, his brown eyes looking even murkier.

Reaching across the table, her father squeezed the top of her arm. "I think L.A. is making you skinnier. You know most guys like a little meat on the bone." He smiled to show he was teasing.

She swatted his hand away and rolled her eyes. "I'm the exact same size I was before I moved. And something with meat would be great. I'm *starving*," she said with a flourishing sweep of her arms to her stomach. "What's good here?"

"The fried pickles are," a voice said from behind her. A very, *very* familiar voice. "So's the poutine."

She turned, taking in the man who towered over her. Dark-colored jeans, a blue T-shirt—tight and displaying an array of ripples beneath it. Stubble covered his jaw, stubble she remembered grating against her skin—

Oh, jeez, had the heater suddenly turned on?

"But I have to admit," Declan continued, his eyes zeroing in on her, "you don't look like you'd eat either of those. You're from L.A.?"

"Mel," her father interrupted, jiggling the ice in his empty glass, "this is the Masquerade's newest addition, Declan Waterford. He's got very talented fingers."

A wave of heat stretched up from her belly and images

of what Declan's fingers could do flooded her brain. This afternoon, just a simple caress on her arms had had her straddling him. What kind of mess would she be if he touched her...somewhere else?

The piano, her father was talking about his fingers playing the piano. No matter, her eyes fell to those fingers. Long. Slender. Hanging at his sides and biting into his palms just a bit. Was he nervous? And was it because of her? Or was it the man sitting across from her—the VP he was hoping wouldn't find out about his ad-libbing antics? The same man he wanted to persuade that the Parrot Lounge was a better slot for him?

Her father set his glass down with a *thunk* loud enough to get the waiter's attention and looked up at Declan. "She's been there long enough for me to try to convince her to leave and join me here."

It was more than hope in her father's voice. Determination. And it thrust a nauseating wave through her.

You're a grown woman. You make your own decisions, including where you live and whom you work for.

Unless she failed at this internship... Her mind wouldn't let her forget about that part.

She shook her head against her father's comment and raised her chin to meet Declan's eyes. Under the light, they gleamed a crystal-like green. Right, he'd asked her a question. "I moved to a small town outside L.A. after college," she said, resisting the urge to look at his lips. She scowled playfully. "And I would too eat those." Whatever they were.

Near the door, the group of girls shuffled in and made their way toward the bar, eyes all on the man who stood beside her table. Skirts rode higher, tongues licked their overly glossed lips. Giggles. Flirtatious smiles.

Declan glanced once at them then suddenly swept Melody's hand into his. "It was nice to meet you...*Mel*."

Melody. It was Melody to him, she wanted to say, but that would have required her mouth to work, and at that moment, with his warm hand cradled around hers, speaking seemed impossible.

And then it hit her—why was he pretending not to know her? Pretending they hadn't shared the most passionate kiss she'd ever had only hours before?

Because he's trying to win over the boss. Not you, dummy.

Melody tugged up a stiff smile, squeezing his hand once. "Nice to meet you, too, Mr. Waterford." Exacting. Not sugar sweet at all. Then she turned her back to him and faced the approaching waiter. Her mind had gone over this before; he wasn't in this for her. So why did his words prickle so much?

She inhaled a slow breath. Vegas and the exhaustion of the conference was messing with her mind. That, and she was on edge because her father was obviously up to something.

By the time her father was done ordering her food and a refill for himself, the looming presence behind her disappeared. He hadn't gone far, though. A piano bench scraped across the wooden platform and speakers in the room buzzed with the microphone's power. The girls tittered like a flock of birds from the bar, then massed to the tables nearest the stage, their heels clacking and tapping.

Melody tried not to take notice of the voice that came over the microphone, welcoming the crowd—the girls—telling them it was time to get the party started. And she tried even harder to ignore the song that suddenly filled the room, Katy Perry's "California Gurls."

She focused on her father, wrapping her hands around the cold water glass in front of her. "So what was so important that you couldn't tell me at breakfast?"

"A father can't want to have a drink and catch up with his daughter?"

She couldn't tell him what Declan's boss had said this afternoon—that her father was planning to turn the hotel over to her. He'd only question why she was in the lounge during off hours, and then she'd have to explain what she was doing with Declan.

Mentally, she shook her head to banish the image of that kiss. The lessons—she'd meant the lessons. *What is that man—heroin?*

Her father knew about her disability, obviously. He'd been there when she was a kid, learning to read and write. But it was her mother who had helped her through college—her father had already relocated to Vegas by that time. And if she admitted she was struggling with her internship—her future career—he'd have all the more weight to try to get her to stay.

Melody sipped her water. "We both know after three days of staying in your hotel, we're all caught up, Dad."

"My hotel…" he mused, tapping his index finger on the rim of his glass. "You know, with your father being vice president of hotel operations, technically, this is your hotel, too."

He didn't own the hotel. His comment was ridiculous. But still, her chair suddenly felt too hard. "And you know I don't want anything to do with it." She hadn't meant to sound so punitive, but she'd had this conversation with him a hundred times and he simply didn't get it. His downcast eyes proof. "Not that there's anything wrong with the hotel.

It's just not...me. Not my dream." Her ordinary, simple life was perfectly ordinary and simple, and there was no way she was going to trade that for the chaos of Vegas. She tucked her hands under the table and wiped her clammy hands on her shorts.

Her father nodded, his mouth stretched into a thin line. "There's a lot of money to be made here."

Melody stiffened and tried to keep her voice casual, even though he was going there again. "I already told you, money isn't what I'm after."

"Evidently," he said with a bursting chuckle. His gaze skated over her outfit, measuring her cutoff denim shorts and worn shoes. A hot surge rushed into her face as he added, "Is there *any* money in publishing?"

Of course there was. At least... she thought so; she'd never actually researched the salaries of editors. "I don't think I'll be living on the streets," she threw at him, the urge to storm out like a teenager budding more and more. Her feet itched in her shoes. Hands fidgeted with her napkin. "Can we please not talk about this again?"

He took a long pull from his drink. "I just think you'd be happier here."

"I'm not moving to Vegas, Dad. End of conversation."

"I already have a house for you. Two bedrooms on a golf course. Only a ten-minute drive from here. It would be perfect."

God, could the man be any more relentless?

"You bought a house for me? You've got to be kidding."

"Not kidding." He grinned, relaxing into his chair. "Small and simple, just the way you like."

Simple. Why had he said that? *Simple, simple, simple.*

Because he knew it would draw her in? Or because it was another slam about her choice of profession?

It didn't matter either way. The fact that he'd purchased a house for her at all—without asking—had her blood boiling.

She pushed away from the table, straightened her shirt, and swiped her hair from her face. "I'm suddenly really tired." Stepping once toward the door, she tried not to scream. "And not hungry. I'm going to my room. I'll talk to you tomorrow."

The song ended. The audience cheered. And she rushed out the door without another word. The hotel air clogged her lungs: nicotine and alcohol and a muddle of heady perfumes. Fresh air—would it be so difficult to pump some fresh air into this place? Declan's husky voice sounded through the thick wooden door, though she couldn't tell what he was saying. Introducing his next song, most likely.

She felt like she was going to explode. How hard would it be for her father to accept that she wasn't going to follow in his footsteps? That she didn't want to be anywhere near Vegas? Not even on a golf course in a small, simple house! With tears drowning her eyes and the expansive, store-lined hall swirling bright colors like a kaleidoscope, she leaned against the wall beside the window of a purse boutique and closed her eyes. Just for a second. Just long enough to ensure she wasn't going to leave mascara streaking down her face before she made her way back to her room. One deep breath. Then another—

"One song," someone said—Declan. Was it crazy that she could recognize his voice so quickly? Body heat tickled the skin on her arms, and all of a sudden she was unsure if she could open her eyes. See him in her bubble. Fall headfirst into those eyes again. "Was I that horrible?"

Her eyes shot open. She looked up. He was so *tall*. She hadn't realized how tall he was, but now that he was standing in front of her, his chest just inches from her—filling her entire view with it as if she were looking through a telescope that blocked out the rest of the world—he seemed really tall. Like if he were to wrap his arms around her right then, her ear would press against that chest, right over his heart. His cheek would rest easily on top of her head.

If he were to kiss her, she'd have to tilt her face up to meet his—

Oh…she was doing it again.

She needed to stop that. And she needed her chest to quit doing that strange fluttery thing.

Forcing a weak smile, she shook her head. "No, you were great. I love Katy Perry. And I love that song. I just…" *I just what? Found out my father doesn't believe I can have a career in publishing?* Yeah, Declan didn't need to know everything behind that. He was standing before her for one reason, and only one reason. A promotion. "I'm tired," she finished, smoothing her hair out of her face.

He didn't nod. Didn't acknowledge her words at all. His lips pressed together, and he watched her, those intense green eyes digging like fingers into her nerves. Every. Single. One.

She held her breath, and after a long minute, his brows pinched together and he said, "Your father upset you." Not a question. And the directness of it pressed in on her like an entire bookshelf leaning on her chest.

Yes, her father had upset her. And purchased a house for her. And she didn't know how else to get it through his head that she didn't want *that*. Any of it.

She blew out a breath, pushing her backside farther into the wall to put more space between them. To be able to take a new breath that didn't smell entirely like him. "I'm fine. We just keep disagreeing on something."

"The Parrot Lounge?" He stood completely still, his hands at his sides, shoulders leaning toward her just the slightest bit, as if the answer to this question was the very source of life. Oxygen and blood, and was that what he'd thought? The meeting with her father was to discuss *him*?

And why did his face look so pained, yet filled with utter hope, as he waited for her to answer? It was more than a drive to be successful. There was something else…something that stole the breathtaking gleam from his eyes. She cocked her head to the side and asked softly, "Why do you want that slot so badly?"

Silence blossomed between them, as much as it could in the middle of a crowded hotel. He leaned in closer, the stiffening of his body starting in his hands and zipping up the muscles in his chest and to the cords of his neck. "Because," he said, more in a growl than a whisper, "rewinding time isn't fucking possible." Something unspoken darkened in his eyes.

She winced against his coarseness. *Why would he…?* She had no idea what he meant by that, but he didn't give her the time to ask. He glanced to his watch and then over his shoulder to the entrance of the bar. "I should get back."

Four little words—*I* and *should* and *get* and *back*—and the disappointment pricked at the base of her throat. She felt different around him. Completely unnerved, yet at the same time warm and wishing she had the guts to reach up and trace the divot between his brows with the tip of her finger. Wipe away his…whatever emotion that was drifting over his features.

A moment passed and then his hand shot out, fingers lingering ever so close to her belly. Dizzy, his nearness made her dizzy. "Let me have your phone," he said, gentler now and extending his fingers even closer.

She inhaled sharply and handed it over, watching as his fast fingers moved along her screen, because holy heck, she wasn't expecting that. A few seconds later the phone in his pocket chimed, and he glanced down at her with a small grin. "We should meet at my place tomorrow for your lesson. I texted you the address."

His place? As in house? Or apartment? Where would someone like Declan Waterford live? To her, he seemed like the type to live at the hotel, and suddenly seeing him outside the Masquerade was all she could think about.

"And…" Unexpectedly, he reached up between them and pressed the pad of his thumb to the center of her lips. "…don't let me near these again."

Declan cleared the piles of junk off the small wooden table near the kitchen. Newspapers, magazines, bills… *It's like a giant-sized mail drop.* Not that he was trying to impress Melody—not in *that* way—but the two of them would need somewhere to talk before the lesson, and his couch was off-limits. Because couches led to sitting close, which led to kissing and other activities he wasn't allowed to do. Not until Brendan was better.

"You've been cleaning for twenty minutes," Broadway announced as he entered the room, his brows raised. "What gives?"

Declan shrugged, tucked the stack of newspapers under his arm, and headed for the trash. "A guy can't straighten up every once in a while?"

Broadway opened the fridge and took out a Coke. "He can. Actually, I'd prefer it. But in the two months we've lived here, you've never spent a night off cleaning." The can hissed as he popped the top. "Which means this *student* you're having over must be more than that."

"She's not." Damn, had he said that too quickly? Didn't matter, because even though he was attracted to her—who wouldn't be with that white-blond hair and sun-kissed California skin?—that was all it was. Attraction.

So why had he chased after her last night? He didn't know. Seeing her visibly upset with her father, he hadn't thought twice about leaving the stage to see if she was all right. He shook his head. *Just being a nice guy.*

Broadway smiled against the rim of his can. "You're bringing her here, so that must mean something." Declan shot him a questioning glance and he explained, "You've yet to bring a girl home, piano boy."

Declan glared and jutted his chin toward the door. "Or it means nothing. Weren't you leaving?"

Broadway laughed and grabbed his keys off the counter. "As long as I get to meet her next time."

"There isn't going to be a next time. She's a *student*."

"Who's coming to your home… Do students do that?"

"They do when the piano at work is inaccessible." His cock jumped at the memory of exactly why that was, at the feel of her slender legs straddling his, her hips pressing and releasing. Despite the trouble he'd gotten in, it was probably a good thing Duey came in when he had. His self-control seemed to vanish as fast as his breath when she was near.

"Let me guess," Broadway said, heading toward the door, "you wouldn't do her if you had a bag of dicks?"

That image—of Melody bared before him—seared his brain and drenched him with a sudden burst of lust. Declan tried to laugh away the feeling, though the uncommitted chuckle that came out of his mouth only branded it deeper. He forced a smile. "Wouldn't ride her if she came with pedals."

His roommate opened his mouth for another round when, without warning, a crash sounded from outside their door, followed by a high-pitched "Dang it!"

Broadway flung open the door.

Melody, with an aluminum container in one hand and a six-pack of beer in the other, smiled sheepishly at the mess of spaghetti and red sauce splayed over the cement walkway. "Hi," she said softly, her cheeks flaming red. "I was worried we'd get hungry, so I brought dinner." She scrunched her nose but smiled wider. "Apparently, I'm not coordinated enough to carry everything at once."

Broadway raised one eyebrow at Declan. "Will work for food?"

Declan shoved his roommate's shoulder. "Will work for a roommate who gets the hell outta here."

"Fine." He stepped over the disaster on the ground, offering his hand to Melody. "Jordan Broadway. Best roommate ever."

Declan chuckled. Was this guy for real? He liked

Broadway—the twenty-six-year-old was actually pretty easy to live with, but he'd been right; Declan had never brought anyone home before.

"Nice to meet you," Melody said, adjusting the six-pack under her arm to shake his hand. Quickly Declan stepped forward and freed her of it. Tight jeans and a flowy black top—it was impossible not to notice her body. The curve in her waist and tone of her legs. The flat stomach her top's elastic stretched across.

Don't even start, Waterford. It'll be a long, uncomfortable night if you do.

"You two have fun tonight," his roommate said and took off down the walkway.

Melody gestured to the mess on the ground with her elbow, then held up the spared container. "I hope you like lasagna, 'cause it looks like we're sharing. Sorry."

"Don't worry about it." Declan smiled at her and jiggled the beer. "As long as you share these, too, we're good."

After helping Declan scrape the saucy mess into the trash and hose off the sidewalk, Melody settled across the small table from him. His apartment was nice, from what she could see. Not grandiose or pretentious, more a typical bachelor pad, but it had style. A couch and piano took up most of the living room, both black and contrasting against the stark white walls. A framed photo sat atop the side table in the corner. Declan with his arm around another guy who had the same facial structure, only much lighter hair. As he dished up the lasagna onto two plates, she pointed at the picture and asked, "Your brother?"

"Brendan," he responded with a brisk nod.

"You two look close."

A pause. His posture changed and expression froze, and apparently she'd just hit a nerve. "We were," he answered her, his words sharp and cutting like the double snap of a whip.

"Were?" *Oh, I hadn't thought…*

"He's still alive. Just"—his lips pressed tight for an instant and he inhaled a slow, deep breath—"living in Ireland. I haven't seen him in a while." There was a tightness to his words. Like maybe he wasn't happy to be separated from his brother. He slid a full plate in front of her. "So what'd you do all day?"

Apparently, they didn't talk about his brother.

Her skin grew warm, discomfited by the awkwardness she'd just created and thinking about the disaster her day had been. *Mixed up my boss's PowerPoint slides. Humiliated her in front of the whole staff. You know, the usual.* "It was… okay, I guess. I'll just be happy when this conference is over and I can go back home."

"Which is Sunday?" He cut the pasta with his fork and shoved a bite into his mouth. He looked different today, in a plain white T-shirt and a blue ball cap sitting backward on his head. Less like a performer, more like a normal guy. But still ridiculously good-looking. And still driving her nerves into a tsunami inside her.

She picked at her food and nodded. "Tomorrow's our last meeting. There's a ball tomorrow night, but I don't think I'll go. It's more for the authors and readers and important publishing professionals, not editorial interns. I leave the day after." And then she could go back to messing up in the comfort of her own home instead of face-to-face with her boss. Communicating mostly online, with the occasional conference call for team meetings, made it much easier to hide her mistakes. Not look like a fool.

"And who are you going home to?" Declan asked, his gaze suddenly intense, his fork paused on his plate. If she didn't know any better, she'd think he was more than simply curious. Jealous?

That thought vanished with a sip of her beer. Jealous over her? Right. And she had three arms.

"I don't live with anyone," she answered with another gulp. "You really think I would have…" Her eyes went directly to his mouth. Those lips—the ones that had devoured hers. The ones he said not to let near hers again. The ones she now couldn't stop thinking about.

She was looking at his mouth. Declan's pants tightened. Why the hell couldn't he get that kiss out of his head? And *why the hell* did he want to reach across the table, take Melody's gorgeous face in his hands, and do it all over again?

A kiss was a kiss was a kiss.

He'd kissed plenty of women before coming to Vegas—before the accident—and yet it was like he'd been injected with some serum that had him craving *her*. And only her.

Melody pointed to the stilled fork in his grip. "If you're done, should we get started?" Desperation coated her words. He lifted his fork and tilted his head.

"Why do you want to learn to play the piano here in

Vegas…while on a business trip? A few days is hardly enough time to acquire any skill."

Her lips parted with what looked like the start of an answer, though nothing came out.

He added, "And don't tell me it's a childhood dream. We both know that's bull." At least he did now. Evidently something was weighing heavily on her—on these lessons.

She pushed her barely eaten pasta away. Hardened her stare. "It is," she said.

But in the small amount of time he'd known her, he'd become acquainted with her eyes. And right now, they were hiding something. "Okay," he said and stood. Fine, he wouldn't push it now—the last thing he needed was to upset her to the point of leaving. That didn't mean he wouldn't try later, though. He gestured to the piano in the living room. "After you."

She nodded. He took the dishes to the sink and when he returned to the living room she was bent at the waist, staring at the coin jar on the coffee table. "What's B?" she said, spinning the half-empty glass mason jar around. Damn, why had he left that there? And why had he written "For B" on the lid?

It wasn't like he didn't know what it was for—to remind him every day what he needed to do—but…at least he could've stashed it in his room where she wouldn't have seen it. Asked about it.

He took a breath. *B could be anything. Beer. Books. A vacation to Baja.*

"You said your brother's name is Brendan." She jostled the jar. "Is this for him?"

He joined her in the room and snatched the jar from her

hands, fighting the urge to just tell her about him. He had to admit, getting it off his chest sounded like a goddamn great idea. But he didn't need her sympathy. Didn't want it. "I'm saving for a new toolbox," he spouted, setting the jar on the far table.

Lips puckered, her head fell to the side. "Why is there a B and not a T then?"

He forced a smile and jerked out the piano bench, feeling the burning pinch that always came with talk of his brother. "Why are you being so nosy?"

For just a moment—too long, in his opinion—she stared at him. No expression. No response. It was like she was looking directly into his soul. Then she tucked a long strand of her hair behind her ear and drew up a small smile. "You're right. I am being nosy. I'm sorry."

He caught her wrist as she was lowering to the bench. He didn't miss the tiny gasp from her mouth or the way she tightened like he'd electrocuted her. "Don't be sorry," he said, softening his tone. He hadn't wanted to startle her. Only let her know he was serious. He swiped his thumb over the crease in her wrist, and her arm grew heavier in his hand. Not much, but he knew exactly the effect he was having on her. "Just know," he added, so low it was almost a whisper, "there are things about me I'm not willing to share, okay?"

This close, he could smell her perfume—a light, fresh scent that had him itching to run his fingers through her hair. Take her mouth with his. Damn his starving libido.

"Okay," Melody said quietly. Something like hurt sifted over her features and then she stepped away and lowered to the bench, tilting her chin up to see him better. "And maybe you should know…" She swallowed hard and readied her fingers on the keys. G chord—just like he'd taught her the last time they'd sat side by side. "I was hoping we could get through this lesson without touching."

It wasn't like that was what she'd come here for, so why did her words shock him so damn much? Had he thought they were going to do anything but practice some scales?

Without touching.

Well, at least now they were on the same page. He shrugged nonchalantly. "No touching. I think I can manage that."

Chapter Four

God, he was *everywhere.*

Two days ago this man with the crystal-green eyes and crooked smile was nowhere — completely nonexistent in her plain-and-simple life — and now Declan was everywhere. In her thoughts. Her memories. Even the bubble of space she'd secured around her.

Maybe that was what it was like when a person developed a fascination with someone. One minute you're floating in a universe, no gravitational hold whatsoever. Then the next you're sucked into something with such intense force not even a meteor the size of the sun could knock you out of it. No matter how hard you fought.

The longer Melody sat beside him, listened to his instructions about where to place her hands on the keys, smelled the heady cologne that hit her each time he shifted, the hotter the burn inside her became. Fifteen minutes and she was about to combust.

"It's not about how hard you hit the keys," he interrupted her absentminded practice of chord progression, leaning in closer but careful to not make contact with her in any way. "The keys are like women. They need to be touched gently, caressed until they purr with the perfect...*melody*."

Yeah, the seductive way he was speaking to her hadn't helped either. It was like he was doing it on purpose, saying these things that threw sexual images at her brain. Everything inside her singed with a tingling heat, like she was drifting in a haze of hunger and wishes and wanting. She sucked in a slow breath through her nose. "Maybe you need to show me."

"Which will do no good. Let's do this...I'll point to a key, you touch it. Don't play it right away, though. I want you to stroke it—tease it—first." He cocked his head to the side and grinned.

Stroke? Tease? She grinned back. "Do you talk to all your students this way?"

"You're my one and only student, so apparently I do." He winked at her, then pointed to the first key. Middle C. "No rush. Nice and slow."

She moved her hand up and down the key with barely any touch at all then played it. He pointed to another. C sharp—one of the black keys that stood above the whites. With her thumb and forefinger, she ran her fingertips down its sides, noticing Declan stiffen with the movement.

Huh, was he feeling all ruffled inside, too? She eyed him curiously. Without a change in his tight expression, he gestured to the next key.

Her fingers slid with gentle pressure over the glossy ivory before she played, and, beside her Declan let out a heavy breath and ran his hand through his hair, gripping the back of his neck.

"Everything okay over there?" she teased. "You seem a little...tense." Something about the way her movements were putting this man on edge shot a spark of uninhibited pleasure through her.

"Just peachy," he answered, staring down at her fingers.

Three more keys pointed to, caressed, and played, then she placed her hands in her lap and turned to him, wondering for the briefest of moments if her cheeks were as red as they felt. What she was doing, would she call it flirting? Though she'd had her fair share of boyfriends, she'd never done something so blatantly sexual in front of one before. Or any man.

"I think we should switch roles," she said, her voice trembling in the back of her throat. "I point, you *touch*."

His eyes burned into hers, blazing hot and so intense she felt seared from the inside out. "No."

She frowned. "Why not?"

"Because what good would it do? You watching me?"

Spinning on the bench to face him, she shrugged. "Plenty of people learn from watching. Think about how many instructional videos there are. Aerobics, home improvement, cooking—"

"You're kind of weird," he said, amused. He sat up and rested the inside of his elbow along the top of the piano. "And I'm kinda curious what type of instructional videos you've watched."

Melody giggled. "Yoga, computers, golf."

"Golf?" She was still amusing him; he was still smiling. "Oddly, I'm sorry I missed that."

She crinkled her nose. "I wasn't very good."

For a moment, his gaze searched her face, skipping back and forth between her eyes, doing that profound stare he did so well. With eyes like his, a look like that should be deadly. "All right," he said, placing his fingers deftly along the keys, "I'll give you three keys. And"—he grinned—"if I'm not pleasuring them to your taste, I sure hope you'll speak up."

Did he talk this way in bed? Or was it dirtier, like when he was onstage? Her heart crammed into the back of her throat, and she swallowed, smiling with the confidence that came with it.

One key, two keys, three. She pointed just as he had, and he took his time fingering the smooth ivory before playing it. C, D, E, and then with that confidence, she pointed to her arm. The bare skin just above her elbow that faced him.

It wasn't a scowl, but by the way his eyes narrowed she might as well have called it that. "You already had three." His whispered words did nothing to stop the quiet room from pressing in on her.

Rounding her shoulders back, she retorted, "And maybe I'm no better than the typical woman…always wanting more." She let those words linger for a long second, then slid her pointer finger higher, to her shoulder. "Maybe you'd rather try here first?"

His lips pinched into a line, and his body went rigid, as if he was fighting some internal battle. But his eyes…they contradicted the rest of his face. On fire and scalding her all over. He inhaled a breath and, ever so sluggishly, lifted his arm and traced a barely there path down the inside of her arm. "What are you doing to me?" he asked, not sounding like a question at all.

A hot prickle followed in the wake of his finger, and her lips drew up. *I think the question is, Declan, what are you doing to* me? It took a minute to find the rest of her mind, and once she did she pointed to the other arm. He did the same, moving slower and dawdling in the sensitive crook of her elbow before continuing on to her wrist.

She bit her cheek against a wider smile. This feeling inside her—so uninhibited…so wild—was unlike anything she'd ever felt. Like she was falling and flying at the same time. It made her light-headed. It made the room spin. And it made her crave *more*. She gestured to her neck next, anticipation bringing every cell in her body to attention.

Put your hands on me, Declan. All. Over. Me.

In a slow, unhurried sweep of his hands, he pushed back her hair with the bends of his knuckles, only lightly brushing the skin on her neck. The lack of full contact was disappointing, so she went for something bolder. A place that would either start or end the night.

Her lips.

His eyes darkened. The room suddenly shrank to half its size. "Melody…"

Don't let me near these again. Why had he said that?

All of a sudden, the burst of confidence flowing through her veins evaporated, leaving her only with a big, heaping pile of doubts and a choked feeling in her throat. "Was it so horrible last time?" She sounded weak, and she hated that her question came out that way, but after the day she'd had, was it so much to ask for something to go right? To not make her feel like a complete failure?

"Jesus, no," he answered in a rush. His fingertips pressed into her neck, only for an instant, then slid around her head and into her hair; she felt like his hands were leaving inscriptions on every single part of her he touched. He shut his eyes and tilted his forehead to hers, and was that her breath that suddenly disappeared?

"Then why?" she choked out.

"I'm attracted to you, Melody." With the pad of his thumb, he outlined her lips. "But that's the problem…I don't want to be."

She tried to pull back to gauge his expression, but his hands held her firmly against him. "Because you have a girl-friend?" Why hadn't she thought of that before? Of course he had a girlfriend. Any man as gorgeous as him would.

His thumb moved along her top lip, then the bottom, her chin supported by his other fingers. "No girlfriend."

Her lips parted, a slim breath to try and compete with the beat of her heart echoing throughout her head. "You don't have a girlfriend," she said weakly. "You're attracted to me. But you still don't want to kiss me?"

His entire body stiffened, and he shook his head against hers. "I *want* to kiss you." Green eyes bored into hers. Oh, those eyes. *Breathe, Mel.* "I want to kiss you more than I've wanted to kiss anybody." Warm breath washed over her face. She blinked, and without warning his mouth was a mere sliver from hers, so close that his lips fluttered against hers when he added, "I want to do much more than *kiss* you."

More than kiss… She held completely still as she worked that out in her head.

She'd never had a one-night stand before. Never had any desire to. But things were different with Declan. Aside from the attraction to him, there was something else. Something deeper. Something that wormed in her chest when she could see the pain in his eyes.

It wasn't that she wanted to fix him. But, maybe, she wanted to be the one to take that pain away. Even just for a moment. Just as she wanted him to steal the memory of her horrid day at the conference.

Lifting her chin and settling her shoulders, she inched even closer. *Give him the go-ahead, Mel. It's not like you're buying a house or moving to another state. It's a kiss. And possibly more. That's all.* She smiled. Then nipped his bottom lip. "I want you to do that, too."

His eyes slammed shut, and a very long silence stretched out.

Maybe I shouldn't have said that.

Maybe I should pull away.

Leave.

Unexpectedly, his hands cradled around her head, fingers dipping to the back of her neck, and he pulled her closer. "Fuck it," he whispered, just before he closed the space between them and traced her lips with his tongue.

Wet. Hot. There was no other way to explain it: she came undone.

Without asking permission, she sank her hands into his hair and tugged him even closer, crushing her mouth to his. He held her face firmly, the feel of his skin touching hers slamming a searing-hot burn into her like the pressure of a branding iron, and asked to enter with his tongue.

Her lips parted, and his hands started to move as he kissed her deeper, and she couldn't tell where he was touching her because as soon as her brain caught up to where his hand was, it moved to another spot, scorching her all over again. He took over her mouth, leading the kiss, tasting her mouth, and touching her everywhere and nowhere and anything that happened to fall between.

Oh, God, this felt so good. *He* felt so good. Their tongues moved, sliding against each other, and it was as if an ember kindled into a full-blown flame.

He kissed her hard, insistently, as if he couldn't get enough of her. As if he needed to taste her, to drown in this kiss with her. As if it had been years since he'd last kissed someone and his starving mouth was physically unable to stop bingeing.

And then his brain must've caught up with the rest of him because, abruptly, the kiss came to a halt, Declan pulling away. She gripped his shoulders, panting against his mouth. "Please don't stop."

His eyes—the color of summer grass—burned straight into her. He wasn't shutting her out, wasn't looking away. He shook his head. "Christ, Melody, you make it really hard to."

"So don't."

"I have to."

Heart hammering hard in her chest, she slid her hands up his neck to secure his head close to hers, not let him pull completely away. "You act like there's someone holding something over your head."

His eyes slammed shut. She'd hit the nail on the head.

"Who?"

"Coming to Vegas," he said in a soft whisper, eyes still closed, "was for…business. Not relationships."

She lifted his hand, kissed the tips of his fingers, then flattened it against her collarbone. "Good thing this is a piano lesson, then, and not a relationship." Where had all this confidence come from? It was like being with Declan transformed her into another person entirely. Someone bold. Brave. *Say I'm right, Declan. I'm right, I'm right, I'm right.*

He nodded. Then without a word, he dipped his head and pressed his mouth against her throat, licking a scorching trail along her sensitive skin. She moaned and felt him smile against her neck. "I could get used to that sound," he said, his warm breath fluttering along her jawline. "Maybe I should give piano lessons more often."

Only if you slide your hand down my belly.

Touch me.

Do something, anything to alleviate the throbbing between my legs.

As if he'd just read her mind, his hand slid down her back and hooked behind her knee, yanking her closer until her leg was on top of his and she was practically straddling his thigh. She started rubbing against it and whimpered at the contact.

The kiss deepened. Then, in seconds, he grew even hungrier. Without wasting a moment, he pulled her tighter, wrapping his arms so firmly around her it felt as if he would never let go. If she was honest with herself, she couldn't say she wanted him to. He roamed a hand down her back, cupped her rear. Then he lifted her and set her atop the ivory, a jumble of notes all playing together.

Best scene in Pretty Woman. *Ever.* And now she was living it.

She moaned, reveling in the sensations rocketing through her blood and veins and body at the slightest trace of his fingertips down her thighs. On her knees. Spreading them wider so he could step inside. She wanted that feeling to last forever because it was so exceptionally intense. Like her body was slipping into an alternate level of reality, some realm of desire she'd never felt before.

Control, she needed to gain control. Not of him, but of her heart and its penetrating beat that was ripping through her. It was impossible to find with her thighs spread, his incredibly hard erection, thick and full, doing its job between her legs—even with all the denim between them. As his mouth searched hers, like he was the answer to any and every question she'd ever had.

He was salty and musky, a scent she would crave long after this was over. His tongue swirled wildly in her mouth, his lips crushing hers with such intensity, as if he would disintegrate into ash if he stopped, that she began to lose control.

"Oh," she said, and she started to close her eyes and just let go, let herself feel what he was doing to her.

"Don't close them," he said in a rough, ragged voice, fingering the button of her jeans. "I want you to watch me take these off."

She flushed at his bluntness. And at the way he was watching her as if asking her permission. *I would really like to watch you take these off.* But only if he was going to do something about the agonizing tension his touch had produced. The unexplainable craving that was stealing her mind. She wanted him; she wanted to do this. Her breathing grew stilted and uneven as the feelings built inside her, like electricity crackling through her veins, blistering and wild and charged. Still sitting on the piano, she watched as he awkwardly peeled off her jeans to bare her legs.

Cool air drew up a wave of goose bumps, followed by the warmth of his palms scraping a line over her shins and thighs. Rougher than expected, and she liked it. By the bulge growing against the zipper of his jeans, he must have, too. His hands kept going once they reached her purple lace panties, fingers dipping beneath the hem of her shirt. "This, too," he said, inching those fingers higher and higher. A swarm of bees scattered in her belly, fingertips sliding and pressing and gripping.

The shirt came off easily — *thank you, whoever invented stretchy camisoles* — and then she reached for his shirt, yanking it off almost as quickly. Pleats and ripples and lines... Who knew a piano player would be in such good shape? Tan skin, though lighter than hers, strained over an array of solid muscles. The sight alone had her fingers itching to touch him.

"Dear Jesus, Melody, you are savagely beautiful. Look at your body. It's pure precision."

No one had ever called her savagely beautiful before. It was dark and feral sounding — especially coated with his accent — but exploded something daring inside her. Consent from her body to...completely let go.

Between their bodies, her fingers found his belt then the button of his jeans. Off they came, and then his hands were clasped to her hips, his mouth returned to hers. Fingers slid lower, toying with the lacy edges of her panties, then even farther down to the cotton panel between her legs. One drawn line, back to front, was all it took to unglue her. She whimpered and silently begged him with her eyes to do that again. Then again and again until she was trembling and burning hot as a blue flame. Greedily, his fingers dipped beneath the fabric and a growl from his chest echoed in the room as he did it once more without the barrier. He kissed her with the kind of profound, uncompromising kiss of a man who had to have his woman, and that woman happened to be balancing precariously close on the edge of coming.

She was soaked, but not embarrassed at all. Not when she could only think about finding the release her body was screaming for. "Condom," she said in breathless anticipation. "Do you have a condom?"

"Yeah." He stepped away to reach for his jeans, where he retrieved a foil packet from his wallet.

Feet on the piano bench, she wriggled her body up to the flat, smooth top of the piano. Better access. More room. Getting ready in her room earlier, she would have never imagined hot piano sex on her agenda tonight. The thrill of those words… Yeah, they were worth grinning about.

Declan laughed and used the bench and row of keys to climb on top of her. "The sweet, innocent intern who doesn't like bad-mannered men…" His hand snaked under her and released the clasp of her bra. "Who knew she'd have a wild side. I do have a bed, you know."

"I like it up here." Her panties came off next, and she immediately dropped her knees open for him.

For a long moment, he eyed her hungrily, drinking her in as if he was desperate for what was next. "I want you, Melody. I want to ravage every single inch of your body. But it's okay for us to go slow, if that's what you want." His voice whispered steady and soft, his lips close to her ear. Those words an endearing mix of tender and guy. But that wasn't what she wanted, was it?

No, tonight was just an escape. A way to get her mind off work and out of the dumps of her mistakes. Hot piano sex, not sweet, slow lovemaking. But then why did the idea of that clench around her heart? Was it because he'd said it at the moment his hands were securely wrapped around the small of her back, his bare chest pressed against hers? Or because it was the very moment when she would have believed anything a man told her?

"I want to make you feel good," he whispered into her ear, sucking the fleshy part into his mouth. Buzzing currents of electricity hurtled through her, and every single cell in her body reached for him. Wanted him. Needed him. She was hot all over and tingling everywhere—straight down to her bones—everything singing out to be touched.

She grabbed at his waistband and pushed his boxers off, and then he was naked and stunning and throbbing. She inhaled a bottomless breath and bit her lip. This was going to happen; she was going to have a one-night stand with the man who was using her to get to her father.

But was he? From the penetrating look he gave her as he hovered over her, positioned and ready, condom now on, it didn't seem like that at all. Crazy as it was, it felt like this was more. The start of something.

Then he teased her, rubbing the head of his penis against her, through all her wetness. She gasped—the feeling exactly what she'd been searching for. Better, even. But she wanted more. Wanted all of him. She closed her eyes and ran her hands down his strong back, to his backside, guiding him.

Slowly, he sank into her, hooked his hands behind her thighs, and lifted. She wrapped her legs around him, feeling the solid, firm length of his erection thrust against her aching hot center, and she moaned into his mouth.

"Does that feel good, Melody?"

She couldn't answer. It was as if her brain had cut power and she couldn't formulate words. All she could do was feel. Declan, his skilled hands on her, the taste of him, the awareness of his gorgeous, lean body over hers. A raw, piercing twinge rose deep within her, dizzying her.

Or maybe that was from Declan's mouth. Or his thorough fingers. She didn't know. It was impossible to think. Never had she been that lost that quick. No man had ever made her feel like that. Achy, in need, about to explode.

Tingles lapped over her skin, her limbs unsteady as she gripped him close. She didn't know how much more she could take. She sank her teeth into her lower lip and thrust her hips slowly against his as he circled his thumb around her pebbled nipples in a maddening rhythm.

"Let yourself go," he whispered near her ear. "For me." A delicious line started from her neck and slid down to her breasts. His tongue. Warm and wet and devouring her. Rocking her body, taking him in as deep as humanly possible, she shuddered several times—not knowing how to let go and shout and scream like she wanted to—and panted heavily as she came.

Still shaking, she pressed her head to the solid piano surface, and he clutched her hips with his deft hands and thrust hard, pounding his way toward orgasm. A mangled groan escaped as he tensed and stilled, her name, followed by, "Fuck me. That was amazing."

She giggled despite the burst of vulgarity coming from his mouth and rested her hands on her stomach, not really knowing where to put them now that they were through. *Is saying good-bye going to be this awkward, too?* Observant as Declan was, though, he noticed her uncertainty and lifted her hand to his mouth and kissed each finger. Then he nibbled her knuckle and grinned.

"Next time, gorgeous, maybe we'll make it to the

bedroom."

Next time?

Melody woke to splashes of sunlight on her face, brightening everything behind her closed lids to a vibrant orange. No blackout curtains like in her hotel room, which must mean—

Lying on her side, she opened her eyes. Apartment-white walls, a long wooden dresser, and a large pile of books on top. And where she lay: soft navy-colored sheets, pillows galore, and a muscled body stretched out beside her.

Oh, God, after a few beers and another round of mind-blowing sex with Declan, she must've fallen asleep. In his bed. She rubbed her face. Cue the walk of shame. At least she was in Vegas—with people up at all hours of the day and night, hopefully no one would notice her sauntering in wearing yesterday's clothes.

The night wasn't supposed to go that way—had they played the piano much at all? Her chest caved. *It's going to take a miracle to fix me.* Not a few piano lessons from a man who made her heart climb into her throat.

With him still sleeping beside her, she allowed herself a tiny moment to memorize his features. After today's meeting and one more dinner with her boss and the team, she'd be leaving first thing tomorrow morning. Back to L.A. Back to her own home, where she could listen to Karri call off the internship in privacy. It was only a matter of time before she did.

Short-cropped hair—the color of milk chocolate—cut

close to Declan's ears and swept a straight line across his forehead where a tiny worry line carved into his perfect Irish skin. Worry line... What did he have to be worried about—moving up to the Parrot Lounge?

A ping of jealousy dug at her stomach. *Where to play piano. Must be nice.* No father hell-bent on hassling him into completely rearranging his life. His goals. His *wants.* No wondering when his last day on the job would be or what would become of his future if he didn't succeed.

Under the coma of sleep and wash of sunlight, he had a fingernail-sized scar on his right cheek she hadn't noticed before. She smiled. So Mr. Piano Star wasn't ridiculously perfect after all.

She slid out of the bed, careful not to disturb his side of the mattress, when a hand clamped over her wrist. "Leaving so soon?" he said, his voice low and raspy with sleep.

She whipped around to face him and his lazy morning smile. "Oh, um... I didn't want to wake you." Her nerves, why did he set her nerves into overdrive?

He tugged, and she fell back onto the bed. Closer to him. "No, you woke up regretting what you did last night and were trying to sneak out."

His bare chest hovered over her, those green eyes digging and searching at her face. Her hands all of a sudden itched to touch him again. To run down the length of him—his torso that didn't have an ounce of fat on it. *No.* She shook her head to rid the thought. He was a one-time fling. She wasn't going to see him anymore after today, so she shouldn't torture herself with thoughts like that. Not to mention she was going to be late to her meeting if she didn't get moving right then.

"No...you don't regret it?" Soft fingertips skated up her arm. Chills followed. "Or no, you weren't trying to sneak out?"

Dang, he was doing it again. Melting her with his touch. With that quirked-up eyebrow that both intimidated and intrigued her. "No, I don't regret it," she said. "And yes, I was trying to sneak out. I have a meeting this morning."

"Do you want something to eat first?"

"No, thanks. If I could just use your bathroom to clean up..."

He nodded his chin toward the door at the edge of the room, and a flashback of his naked backside retreating to the tiny room to deposit a condom hit her like a train. The second time with him had been even better than the first. Slower and stretched out on the bed, they'd had more room to explore each other's bodies.

She shifted beneath his rock-hard body. *Is it getting hot in here?*

Unexpectedly, he dropped a kiss onto her cheek and whispered in her ear, "That's the same expression I'm sure I'll get every time I look at my bed now. Picturing your beautiful, naked body lying on it." A smile pushed at his cheeks.

Contagious as it was, his smile didn't draw one out from her. Because tomorrow afternoon she'd be back home and he'd be back to his performances, flirting with the girls on the dance floor.

Lonely. It made her feel lonely.

Chapter Five

"**N**apoleon's?" Heather asked, flopping down onto Melody's hotel bed.

Can't we just stay in so I can finish drafting the first-pass letter to Justine? It'd been such a long day with closing speeches from a few guest speakers, and on top of that Karri had requested she finish writing up notes on one of their newest author's manuscripts so Karri could attend tonight's ball, and that fluffy bed was looking pretty heavenly right about then.

Melody protested with a quick shake of her head. If she was going out, she didn't want it to be Napoleon's. Not anywhere Declan might be. Last night had been a mistake, she realized as she sat through hours and hours of PowerPoints that day. Spending time with Declan at all had. Because what did she have to show for it? Nothing. Well, she knew how to play a few chords, but she was pretty sure that the research on music theory she'd read said she would have to learn how to play an instrument, not press a few notes. Not have hot sex on said instrument, either.

"If we're going to go out," Melody said, balling her long hair into a knot on top of her head, "I'd rather get out of this hotel."

"Dancing?"

Melody screwed up her face. Yeah, no. "Maybe something not so…sweaty. More relaxed. And outdoors. Like a pub or something."

After spending a few minutes searching on her phone, Heather found the perfect place at the Plaza. "*Biergarten*," she said with a giggle. "Sounds like fun."

Thirty minutes later the two of them hopped out of the taxi and paid the driver. Heather gestured to a neon sign: CLUB RAW. "You sure you don't want to shake your ass for a little bit?"

And have strange men rubbing their body parts against her? No, thanks. "I'm sure. Besides, I've never been to a beer garden before."

They entered the gate to the outdoor, courtyard-like area. Spans of grass butted up to a small stage, open stalls selling a variety of food items—kabobs and gourmet fries—scattered between. Vine-covered trellises traversed a large section of grass where a variety of games sat. Bocce ball, Frisbee golf, and—

"Corn hole!" Heather screeched. "I love that game. We *so* have to play."

Melody laughed at Heather's enthusiasm. Maybe a game would get her mind out of the gutter, anyway. Seemed ever since she'd left Declan's, that lonely feeling had only intensified. "Fine," she said. "You go set it up, and I'll get us drinks."

From the craft beer booth, she bought two double IPAs—yeah, the day needed to be wiped away with an insane amount of alcohol—then trekked through the grass to where Heather was standing with two guys. One short and stocky, the other tall and...

Oh, God. What was *he* doing here? Wasn't he supposed to be working?

To think of it, he'd never said so when they'd parted ways earlier that morning. She'd merely assumed he worked every night.

Heather waved her over with a bright smile. "Mel, look who it is. The piano guy!" Then, as if the idea had hit her square in the face, her smile fell and nose scrunched. "Wait." She pointed to Declan. "You were mean to her."

Maybe Melody should have told Heather what she'd been doing last night.

"He already apologized," Melody said, handing over the beer and swallowing her heart down out of her throat. For some reason, her body and mind had different ideas on what they wanted to do with the tight-shirted, muscled man in front of her. Every cell in her body knew what it felt like for him to touch her, to caress her, and was screaming for him to do it again.

But in her mind, she knew...her time with him last night had only been a stress release. Nothing more. How could it be?

Heather's brow crinkled. "He did?" She gave Melody a *when did that happen and why didn't you tell me* sort of look. Not exactly the time to explain, especially with him standing—his head cocked to the side and a smile flirting with his lips—so near.

"Corn hole's more fun when you have teams," Declan's roommate—Jordan, she remembered—interrupted, a plastic cup perched at his lips and his eyes smiling deviously toward Declan. Then he abruptly tugged Heather to the other end of the grass area where the colorful wooden box with holes sat.

"Girls go first!" she screamed. Her friend threw her a suggestive look over her shoulder, then kicked off her heels and got to work collecting the beanbags.

Melody turned to Declan. "What are you doing here?"

He threw his arms out to the sides, a smile widening across his gorgeous face. "A guy can't have a night off with his friend?" He bent to retrieve the beanbags for the girls' team—green, just like his eyes. Darn her for noticing that. He tossed one at her, his gaze skimming over her face. "And play a ridiculous game with a girl who obviously needs a night out, too?"

How could he know that? She wasn't one of those girls who wore her emotions on her face, was she? She straightened and sipped her drink, appreciating the ice-cold stream it ran down her throat when she swallowed. No, she wasn't one of them. He'd just taken a lucky guess based on what she'd told him yesterday.

He tossed another beanbag to her, then stepped into her space and took her cup. "You're up first." His fingers lingered on hers—warm in contrast to the cold of the cup—for a beat of a moment before he retreated with her drink in his hand.

Her mind raced. Should she leave? Go somewhere else and allow Declan and his friend to enjoy this place?

Mentally, she shrugged. It was just a game of corn hole.

They weren't alone, and as good as he looked tonight in those fitted jeans and T-shirt that showed off every crevice she knew existed beneath, she had control.

The two of them took turns tossing the beanbags into the holes across the court, laughing when they missed and cheering when they made it—which was only once, on Declan's throw. "This game is a lot harder than it looks," she said, collecting the bags for another round. Her cup empty, she was feeling a bit more relaxed. She'd even ditched her heels for better stability.

Declan chuckled. "Aiming a round item into a hole? Yeah, I wouldn't expect you to be a pro at that."

She elbowed him. "Do all guys turn everything into a sexual joke?"

The light expression on his face fell along with his hands to his sides. "Not at all. I can be serious." His eyes burned into hers. "Did you talk to your father about the Parrot Lounge yet?"

Her body tensed, her muscles quivering all the way to her toes. "Is that why you're still here? To find out if I can get you the *coveted* Parrot Lounge?" She'd known that was half of their deal, so why did it pierce her chest when he said that?

In a blink, he tracked across the space between them and took her chin gently into his hand. "Melody, even if one of my bosses wasn't your father and the Parrot Lounge was *completely* out of the equation, I would still be here." There was something unspoken in his eyes and maybe even his voice, and it irked Melody that she couldn't put her finger on why that was.

I came to Vegas for business, not a relationship. So he

didn't want a girlfriend, she could understand that. Maybe he was getting over a breakup or something. But to play the same songs over and over for drunken crowds? It didn't make sense to her.

I wish you were easier to read, Declan.

He ran the tip of his thumb across her bottom lip. "I may have not known that you were going to be here tonight, but now that you are I intend to spend every moment of it with you." Yeah, nothing unspoken there. In her reaction, too: the tingles under the fingertip burning. *Why do I become nothing but liquid when he touches me?*

Is it wrong that I want to spend one more night with him?

Hastily, she shook the thoughts away. Spending time with Declan would only be a waste. She looked past him, just wanting to escape the intensity of his eyes. "Why bother?" *And where did my voice go?* "This is my last night in Vegas." And she planned not to come back for a long, long time. Her father could visit her at Christmas. "You'll never see me again."

His thumb dipped into the corner of her mouth and then swept over the line of her jaw. "If this is your last night, then spend it with me." That one finger felt as if it was a hundred hands, feathering along her skin.

She narrowed her stare. "Because you want me to talk to my father?"

"Because"—he leaned closer and whispered into her ear—"all I can think about is how amazing you made me feel last night. How your body felt against mine. And even if we don't do *that*"—he paused a moment, to let the memory sink back in—"I'll take anything I can get. Even if it's just this." Then he kissed her, just once, at the edge of her mouth.

Soft, slow, and so, so delicious.

Her insides melted, just like that.

She sucked her bottom lip into her mouth, wanting to taste him again. But there was something she needed to know. "Answer one question first," she said, feeling that burst of confidence he seemed to ignite inside her. His eyes stayed on hers, so she continued. "What was so horrible in Ireland that you left to come sing to belligerent people in a hotel?"

His face paled. His feet shifted. Though she had to give it to him, whatever the reason, he'd clearly practiced looking unaffected. "I owe something to someone," he said in a series of clipped-off words.

Her hand twitched, the urge to reach up and run her fingers over the line drawing across his forehead burning at her fingertips. She wanted to ask him if that was why he had a coin jar, and why he'd kind of panicked when that boss of his had walked in on them and demanded he not work that night. Instead, she slowly nodded, tilting her chin up to meet his eyes. "Okay," she said in return. She would drop it for now, because the night was still young and by the pained look on his face, pressing him would surely end it.

She flattened her hands on his chest then pushed up a smile. "Want to know something else you can learn from instructional videos?"

His eyes searched her face, as if he was trying to figure her out, then his lips pinched into a hesitant smile. "How to amuse an Irish guy with your random activity undertakings?"

Melody laughed, but inside she was suddenly buzzing. That fluttery feeling was back in her chest. How could some-one make her feel so tense and so relaxed at the same time?

She shook her head.

"Hmm, knitting?" That look, with his smile widening and his eyes brightening, did something funny to her belly. She pressed her hand to her middle because *he makes me feel gooey inside when he looks at me like that.*

She shifted her stance, the cool grass tickling the sides of her bare feet, and wrinkled her expression. "I wasn't very good at that one, either."

He reached between them, pried her hand from her stomach and sandwiched it in between his. "I won't hold that against you. My grandma once told me that only trolls with really big hands can knit." He squeezed her hand. "Obviously, she couldn't knit, either."

Warmth seeped in through her skin and climbed up to her wrist…elbow…higher, higher, higher. She wanted to be closer to him. Wanted to feel more of him. Her eyes flickered past his shoulder to the club across the street. "Let's go dancing."

D eclan's cock jumped. Damn, every time Melody ground her ass against it, it was like an electric shock to his gut. It wasn't the tight jeans that clung to that ass. No, it was remembering what was beneath them. What her smooth skin felt like under his hands. Her warm wetness that he'd sunk into over and over and over.

He wanted her again.

But wanting her was wrong.

This was the war his mind had been fighting for the last five songs.

More like since the moment you first laid eyes on her.

One more night was all he had with this unbelievably gorgeous girl, and he was going to make damn sure he didn't waste it. Not because of the Parrot Lounge. He'd meant what he'd told her earlier—that even if trying to get a promotion was out of the picture, he would still be standing right where he was, with his hands sliding down the length of her sides, feeling her toned stomach muscles beneath the thin purple top she was wearing. At his touch, she spun, wrapping her arms loosely around his neck. "What's your grandma like?" A hint of sweet vodka hit his nose.

Immediately, he warmed, like a fleece blanket had been draped over his shoulders. Thoughts of Grams always did that to him. He held Melody close to him, shifting from foot to foot along with her movement, and raised an eyebrow. "You really want to spend our last night together talking about an old lady who couldn't knit?"

She shrugged, sliding her fingers through the hair at the back of his neck. "I just want to know more about *you*."

Eight little words. How could they hit him as hard as a freight train, then?

He straddled her legs with his and tightened his grip around her waist. Fine, it wasn't like talking about Grams would reveal anything about the type of asshole he really was. "My parents died when I was ten. She—"

"Both of them?" Melody interrupted, leaning back with a crumpled expression.

He nodded. "Car accident. Grams took over and raised my brother and me. Between the two of us, she had her hands full. We were a little reckless in our teenage years." After that, too. Though if he said that, he wasn't sure he could hide the emotion that would surely come along with talking about what he'd done to his brother. "She passed away two years ago."

A small gasp escaped her parted lips, and he could tell by the sympathetic twist of her features and the soothing way she was stroking his head what she was thinking. He'd lost his parents. And his grams.

And that was only the start of it. The unsaid words—the explanation about his brother—crashed like wrecking balls in his brain. They wanted out, too. But what was the point? It wasn't like he was going to see Melody after tonight, anyway—no matter how much he'd want to.

"She lived a good, full life," he told her, toying with the back hem of her shirt. It was true; Grams was just shy of eighty-five when she passed. She'd worked as a nurse, raised children and grandchildren, and died with a smile on her face.

Unexpectedly, Melody tightened her hold on the back of his head and crushed her lips to his. As good as it felt to finally have her lips back on his, to feel this pressure and breathe in her scent, he didn't need a pity kiss. Didn't deserve one.

"Don't," he said, pulling away just enough to look her in the eyes.

She blinked. "I just—"

"You feel sorry for me." He shook his head, trying to swallow down the anger clawing at the base of his throat. "Don't."

She stared at him, not protesting what he'd just said in any way, which was good. There was already one liar in the group, and he didn't need another one. They stared at each other for a long moment, the beat of the music thumping loud and hard just like his heart. Then her hands circled around his neck and smoothed over his jaw. "This isn't a pity kiss," she said, easing toward him slowly. "This is an *I want to feel you inside me again* kiss." The distance between them disintegrated, and it took his body a moment to catch up with his brain trying to work out her words.

Declan wound his arms around the small of her back and pulled her closer—his entire front side crushing against her entire front side. "Well," he said into her mouth, "maybe we should do something about that. I think my piano misses you."

She giggled and opened her eyes—glazed from a few drinks and pupils blown out to their rims from the tingly tension she must have been feeling, too. "There's a Jacuzzi tub in my hotel room I'd like you to get acquainted with."

White-hot heat, along with a rapid slideshow of images that involved their naked bodies in a hot tub, momentarily overtook his body. "What about your friend?" His fingers were already itching to start pulling her toward the exit.

"She's not staying with me."

"I mean, should we taxi back with her and Jordan or let them be?"

Melody's eyes followed his to the bar, where her friend and Broadway were laughing, shot glasses in hand, ready to shoot back the golden liquid. "Looks like they'll be just fine. We'll text them from the car."

If ever there was a torturous taxi ride, this had to be it: Melody's body propped next to his. Darkness surrounding them. Her lips trailing a warm, wet line up his neck. Carefully he shifted, adjusting the pressure against his zipper. Or attempted to, anyway. Seemed the longer he sat next to her, the more swollen he became. It felt like he was going to explode before they reached Las Vegas Boulevard.

Melody closed her lips around the fleshy part of his ear and moaned.

That was it; he couldn't take it anymore. Gone was the worry about what the driver might think. He had to taste her. Now. And if he couldn't strip her down and take her between the legs, then he'd have to make do.

His hand snaked around her head, guided her mouth to his, then he parted her lips with his tongue. Declan kissed her deeply, tracing her lips with his. She ran her fingers through the back of his hair, down to his shoulders, and damn, those jeans growing tighter and tighter. He pulled away slightly, silently pleading with his eyes that she ride the hell out of him.

Impishly, she smiled, twisted her body, and swung a leg over the both of his. A quiet giggle as she sank low onto him to avoid being spotted in the rearview mirror—almost as if she was embarrassed but trying not to be. With her heat this close to his aching dick, it took everything he had to keep his hands away from the button on her jeans. Once he went there, he knew there would be no stopping him. Instead he slipped his fingers beneath the hem of her shirt. Skin on skin. Not much, but a hell of a lot better than where they'd been a moment ago. Farther up, he outlined the material of her bra, occasionally knuckling over the thin pad where her nipples puckered beneath.

Her fingers dug into his back with need and fervor, a low, almost inaudible sigh drifting from her lips to his. Sweet agony, was this the world's longest taxi ride? He nipped at her lip, took her for one more intense kiss then, thankfully, the taxi came to a stop.

The driver turned around, not altering his expression at all when seeing Melody straddling him. Melody moved to climb off, but Declan held her tight. "You're not going anywhere," he whispered and then paid the driver.

With her still attached to him, he shimmied out of the backseat and stepped into the Masquerade Hotel. She tightened her legs around his waist, giggling as they passed group after group of vacationers, foreigners, conference goers. "Declan, this is my father's hotel. What if one of the employees recognizes me?"

He lifted a brow. "Recognize the daughter who, up until a few days ago, was nonexistent?" A question mark fell over her expression. Yeah, he'd done a bit of research on her, too. Nothing but a few questions to some of the higher-ups, though enough to know she hadn't been to the Masquerade in years. He winked at her. "I think your chances are pretty slim."

"You've been asking about me?"

"Only because I wanted to make sure I wasn't taking on a psychopath as a student." He smirked, and sidestepping a booth filled with all sorts of women's stockings, started toward the casino, which they would have to cut through in order to get to the room elevators.

Her face twisted, and he could tell by the look on it that she was wondering if it was really because of her father and the slot at the Parrot Lounge. She was partly right.

"Or maybe I was trying to figure out what it is you and your father disagreed about since, you know, you've been kind of secretive about it." As if he should be talking…

She straightened, her back stiffening. "Not because you were trying to take a different angle in getting me to talk to him?" A breath, and then: "Look, Declan, that was part of our deal. There's no guarantee that you'll get the Parrot Lounge, because I don't exactly have any say in the matter. But I'm going to talk to him. Right now if you'd like."

He was shaking his head when all of a sudden Melody's eyes widened like she was seeing the ghost of a long-lost relative.

"My boss," she clipped out, wiggling under Declan's tight grip. "Oh my gosh, she's coming this way!"

He started to release her. "Do you want to go talk to her?"

"What?" Clinging to his neck, she buried her face into his shoulder and whisper shouted, "*No!* She can't see me like this! I've been drinking, and I'm wrapped around…you. Just go!"

Laughing, he started through the casino, but froze when he heard the woman shout Melody's name.

Melody's entire body stiffened like that one word jolted her with a bolt of lightning. Fingers dug into the back of his neck, and her chest stilled as if she'd sucked in a breath and held it.

"Do you want me to run?" he asked into the side of her neck, not at all teasing. A silent moment passed—quick with the blink of an eye but enough time for the woman to close the space between them—then Melody slid her body off

Declan's and straightened her shirt.

"Hi, Karri."

The woman — older and wearing way too much makeup — approached, her hands fixed to her hips, fingernails poking into the satiny red material of her long dress. She cocked her head, looking once up at Declan then back to Melody. "I know you've never been to a conference before, but this is not the place to be flaunting your one-night stands."

Melody opened her mouth, likely to apologize, based on the frown covering her face and the position of her slumped shoulders, but the woman — Karri — continued.

"This hotel is littered with industry professionals, and if one of them recognized you from any of our workshops, it would look bad. Really bad. For our company and for me." She shifted her feet, then planted them wider and said with an exaggerated sigh. "Please tell me you at least finished drafting the letter to Justine?"

Melody's eyes widened, and Declan didn't like the way seeing her upset tugged at something deep inside his chest. By the look on her face, she obviously she hadn't finished. Maybe it was the way Melody was crumbling beneath this woman's icy glare, or maybe it was the demeaning tone of her voice…whatever it was, that tugging in his chest was quickly morphing into a hot, sharp prick at the base of his throat.

"I…" Melody began, still fingering the hem of her shirt.

Karri's overly lipsticked lips pinched into a thin line. "You didn't. You do realize I need to send that to her tomorrow morning in order to make December's release…"

Melody threw up her hands, palms out as if in surrender. "The night sort of got away from me, but I'll have it done and to you in a few hours. I promise." She looked at Declan, her eyes flaring with panic. Whatever this letter was she was supposed to have finished, it was probably something that would take much longer than a few hours. And now her boss was pissed.

Declan stepped closer to Melody. "It's my fault. Mel didn't want to go out, but I forced her to."

Karri let out a harsh-sounding chuckle. "I'm pretty sure Melody is a grown woman who can make her own decisions."

Melody eased closer to her boss, throwing a look to Declan that screamed he needed to shut up. "Yes, I am, and I can. If you just give me a few hours I'll have it to you."

Karri eyed Melody, flicking her stony gaze over her entire body then focusing on her face. "You've been drinking, so don't bother." She jutted her chin into the air. "It would probably be crap I would have to redo, anyway."

That did it. Declan had no idea who this woman thought she was—or even *who* she was—but he was speaking before he could stop himself.

"Who are you to tell her what she writes will be crap? Regardless if she's had a few drinks, I happen to know she's smart and witty and completely capable of writing whatever fucking letter you throw at her."

"Declan, no," Melody said quickly, gripping his arm. He inhaled a shallow breath and clasped his hand around hers.

"Yes," he said to her. "This woman is treating you like dog shit, and you don't deserve it."

"This woman is my *boss*!" she whisper shouted then whipped her head back to Karri. "I'm sorry. I—"

"Don't apologize to her. Being your boss gives her no right. But it looks like she's trying to, one, take advantage of you because you're letting her, and two, be a bitch in the process."

The two women gasped at the same time. Shit, was that a line he shouldn't have crossed?

"Security!" Karri all of a sudden shouted, waving her arms wildly into the air. "Security, this man is threatening me!"

"Declan!" Melody sucker-punched his arm.

"Security, security, security!"

"No," Declan rushed out. *Fuck.* What had he done? He was only trying to stick up for Melody since she wasn't. She didn't deserve to be talked to that way—

Two uniformed guards suddenly flanked him. "Seriously?" he said to the both of them. "I work here."

"We need you to come with us," the taller of the two said. Declan didn't recognize either of them and was suddenly regretting not ever paying attention to any of the staff. They looked at Melody. "You, too."

Chapter Six

"I am *so* mad at you right now." Melody plopped down into the chair on the opposite side of the room from Declan.

They'd been in the holding room for well over an hour, staring at the creamy beige walls and burlap carpet and not speaking at all.

Declan opened his eyes and connected them with Melody's. He'd been sitting against the wall on the floor, his head leaned back and eyes closed, for at least the last twenty minutes. "You're talking to me now?"

She scowled at him. "Only because I can't stand this silence anymore. How long do you think they're going to keep us in here?"

He smiled, though there wasn't any feeling behind it. "Well, if you want to tell me off again, I'm sure there'll be time for that."

She had told him off—on the escorted walk back to

security headquarters. And after the security guards ignored her demand to get her father in the room. And especially after Declan had told her that if she'd visited Vegas more, they probably would've recognized her as the VP's daughter and let them go by now.

Still, that didn't stop the flare of heat from returning to her chest. "You called my boss a *b* word."

He zeroed his gaze on hers. "No, I said she was being one, and she was. *To you.* And I didn't like it."

Oh. Something about those words—and the possessiveness in his voice when he said them—cut through the angry clench her muscles had taken on. "Why?"

He brought his knees in close to the rest of him and folded his arms across the top of them. "I've seen you with that woman twice now, and it's apparent in the way you act around her that she's got some sort of high-and-mighty shit she's pulling with you. Putting you down to build herself up."

Melody shook her head, the exhaustion of the last hour weighting down her whole body. The realization that Declan had it all wrong, too. "She's not putting me down to make herself feel better. She's putting me down because I completely deserve it after all the mistakes I've made while working with her."

He lifted an eyebrow. "She's your mentor, right? And you're an intern? Doesn't that give you the right to mess up and her *not* the right to blame you for it? Or take it out on you?"

He hardly knew her, and yet he was trying to protect her, and knowing that completely obliterated the rest of her anger. She rubbed her hands over her face and sucked in a deep breath. "Maybe, but…I don't think she was expecting to be dealing with so many mistakes when she decided to take me on. I probably hold the record: most mistakes *ever*. It's why I asked you to teach me to play piano."

His lips pursed, and just as she realized that likely made zero sense to him, he said, "I have no idea what that means."

Yeah, a few months ago she wouldn't have, either. She crossed the room and sat on the floor in front of him, folding her legs like a pretzel and intertwining her fingers on her lap. "There's a theory that learning to play a musical instrument will help the brain learn rhythm development, which is linked to reading and writing difficulties in people with dyslexia." She cringed at that last word. It wasn't a word she said out loud to people often.

"The mistakes…" He lowered his legs and leaned forward, elbows on his knees. "You're dyslexic?" The question was soft, not filled with repulsion or sympathy or any other emotion she imagined him having. Not even understanding, which she was most grateful for. She didn't need him pretending to know what she was going through.

She nodded. "Research says that people like me will often work in a job that is well below their intellectual capacities." Pressure constricted around her chest. "I don't want to be a part of that statistic. But I guess it's there for a reason. My brain just doesn't work like a normal one."

Declan laid his hands over hers and chuckled softly. "You, not normal? You're kidding, right?"

The pressure tightened, like all four beige walls were toppling one by one over her. Crushing her. "Do normal people trip over words a third grader could read? Or misspeak words like 'basgetti' in front of a table full of publishing professionals?" It wasn't the least of it, but she knew if she went on, giving him more and more humiliating pieces of her, the sudden prickling in the corners of her eyes would turn to full-on tears.

He watched her for a moment, his eyes drifting back and forth between hers and the thumb that was sweeping over her wrist. "So that night at the bar," he said quietly, his accent almost completely disappearing with the softness of his voice, "when you requested that song, your stuffiness was more of a way to cover up...that?"

"Stuffiness?" She frowned. "I was not being stuffy. I was—"

"Requesting a song that I couldn't—without feeling like I was going to hell—add words to. You wanted me to stop cussing, and there's nothing wrong with that. I'm just thinking maybe there's more of a reason for it."

More of a reason... Right, he didn't know about that, either. She sighed heavily. "Remember what your manager said that day he walked in on us? That I was the one who my dad wanted to hand over the hotel to?"

Declan lifted a smug smile. "You mean that day you couldn't handle this"—he swept his hands in front of his chest and face—"and attacked me with your mouth?"

God, that smile. It pulled at her, pulled her closer and closer to him. Until, that was, his words registered. She nudged him with her foot. "That is *not* what happened." At least she didn't think so. Her cheeks grew warmer. "But yes, that day. And remember why I ran out of the bar that night I was having dinner with my dad?"

His fingers slowly crept up her arm to the crook in her elbow, his eyes locked on hers. "You said you kept disagreeing about something."

She nodded. "He wants me to manage the hotel. He even

bought me a house out here for when I fail my internship."

"He thinks you're going to fail? Why?"

"If you were to look at the research," she said, shrugging, "it's obvious I'm going to." She ticked off the reasons one finger at a time. "Reliance on others for written correspondence; frequently has to reread sentences in order to comprehend; uncertainty with words, punctuation, and spelling…"

"It's only research," he quipped back, his shoulders flexing beneath the material of his shirt. "I'm sure every person is different."

"What my father doesn't know is that research also says people with dyslexia have a lower success rate and difficulty maintaining a successful business. I'm sure if he knew that, he'd be rescinding his offer in a heartbeat." She couldn't help the derisive tone of her voice.

"Seems to me," Declan said, cocking his head and wrapping his fingers all the way around her arm, "you need to lay off the research." His voice was harder now. Protective. He tugged her arm until she was face-to-face with him, his eyes just as firm as his voice. "Reading all that shit is scaring you into not believing in yourself. Not looking past what you can't do or what you have a hard time with to see what you can do. Or even what you want to do."

Melody closed her eyes, needing to distance herself from the deep pull of his eyes.

His breath, followed by his words, brushed softly against her ears. "What is it you *want* to do?"

Up until this very moment, she'd wanted to pursue a career in publishing. Wanted to work with books and words and the magic of them, despite her difficulties. But was

Declan right about her being scared of what she couldn't do? *Was* she scared?

And was that why she despised the hotel life? Because inside she knew she couldn't ever live it?

No. There were other things, too. Like—

Declan's fingers drew a gentle line down the side of her face. Along her jaw. Then splayed out like a fan against her neck.

She opened her eyes. "That's not fair. You ask me a question and then distract me so I can't think of an answer."

"A question like that you shouldn't have to think about."

Just the lingering effects of the alcohol. If he asked her again tomorrow, she'd be able to answer much quicker. She was sure of it.

She reached up between them and dragged the tip of her finger over his lips. She grinned. "Guess that means you can go back to distracting me then."

Not knowing how to explain the way Melody's features had twisted when he asked what she wanted to do with her life…and how seeing her waver like that, all because of some stupid research, clawed at his heart, Declan wrapped his hand around the back of her neck, pulled her in close, and pressed his mouth to hers.

She brought her hands up and slid them through his hair, brushing her thumbs across his cheeks. His tongue dipped between her lips—a small taste, though there was no way he'd only be able to take just one. He commanded her mouth, stroking his tongue along hers, and her hands skimmed his neck, shoulders, chest as she leaned into him, pushing her tongue deep into his mouth. His fingertips traced the line of her jaw, down to her collarbone. He slid them around the curve of her back until he reached her irresistible ass—

The door swung open. "Apparently Declan Waterford isn't just good with his fingers," someone spouted from the opening.

Her dad. Shit.

And the VP of the hotel. Double fucking shit.

Melody pulled away and scrambled to her feet, straightening her shirt and hair, then cleared her throat. "Dad, hi." She smiled, though even Declan could tell it was forced and unnatural. "Um…your security guards didn't believe that I was your daughter."

Mr. Sumner stepped farther into the room, his black loafers scuffing silently against the carpeting. He tucked his hands into the pockets of his gray suit jacket and threw his shoulders back. "They know now. Every single one of them," he said to her, backing against the door to open a space just the size of Melody for her to move through. "I think it's time you go back to your room." The way he looked across the room at her the way a father would—protective and maybe somewhat caring—didn't match the clipped manner of his words. And by the way Melody didn't flinch one bit, she must've been used to it.

Melody glanced back to Declan, her hand twitching as if she'd wanted to reach for him but then thought better of it. *Good choice, Mel, since now that he's looking my way there are daggers in his eyes.*

"Mr. Waterford, I'd like a moment with you," Mr. Sumner said to him.

Melody's eyes bulged. "No, Dad, he didn't do anything. My boss Karri was drunk and overreacting and—"

"It's okay," Declan told her, nodding his chin toward the doorway. "I'm sure he just wants to hear my side of the story."

It took her a moment—her eyes searching Declan's face for some sort of clue that he was fine—but Melody eventually surrendered to her father and left the room.

The door's *click* echoed throughout the bleak room, triggering an immediate change in Mr. Sumner's stance.

Hands out of his coat.

Finger pointing at Declan.

This isn't going to be good.

"I'm not sure what the hell happened down in my casino," he spit out, narrowing his eyes, "but I do know that I have a customer complaint against you, including several witnesses that claim you verbally threatened this woman."

Declan knew how business guys like him were. The customer was always right. It was good business. So he didn't even try to explain what had happened. Besides, based on what Melody had told him about her father, it was likely he wouldn't care one bit that Declan had been trying to stick up for *her*.

Mr. Sumner continued. "I'm taking you off shows for an entire week, starting tomorrow."

No shows? "Hold up." Declan threw his hand up, his heart suddenly suffocating him. No shows meant no pay, which also meant Brendan would have to wait even longer. "You can't do that, sir. I can't go a whole week without pay. I need that money."

"You're lucky I don't fire you for causing a scene in my

hotel." He held his elbows wide from his body, chest thrust out. Declan wasn't sure if the reddening of his boss's face was because he was being challenged or remembering what Declan had been doing to his daughter when he walked into the room. Both seemed a topic he didn't want to breach.

Fine then. "Is that all?"

Mr. Sumner's arm swept out in the direction of the door. "Not unless you can assure me that nothing else of my interest or belongings will be aroused by you."

What kind of request was that? And what kind of guy did he think Declan was?

Declan flattened his palm in the direction of Sumner, hoping he'd be able to contain the sarcasm ready to escape in his voice. "Scout's honor."

As Declan made his way to the exit, one of the security guards who'd escorted him and Melody up to the room burst through the door. "Boss, we have a situation in the ballroom. I think you should hurry."

Both men rushed out, and Declan followed, feeling heavier and heavier with each step down the hallway. He made it to the elevator, pressed the down button, then stared at the wall, wishing he could punch the shit out of it. But there were security cameras, and he really couldn't risk losing more shows.

What the hell was he going to do for money? He couldn't just sit on his ass for an entire week and do nothing when his brother was counting on him.

His phone buzzed in his pocket. He slid it out.

Melody. And what looked to be a room number.

The hotel room door shot open and Melody flung herself into Declan's arms. She buried her forehead into his neck, and just the sweet scent of her started to erase the shitty mood that had begun to infiltrate his every thought on the way to her room. Her warm lips pressed into the skin below his neck and she whispered the word "sorry."

He squeezed her tighter, not wanting to let this feeling go. The very presence of her calmed him on the inside, but when her body was brushing, shoving, scraping against his, it also stirred his blood and heated his veins. Such a mouthwatering combination. "You have nothing to be sorry for."

She eased back, setting her face directly in front of his. "What's the damage?"

The corner of his mouth pulled into a smirk. "Wow, despite the distance between you two, you must really know your father."

"He can be overly cutthroat sometimes," she said, her nose scrunching up. "Please don't tell me he fired you. I wouldn't be able to live with myself if he did."

Declan shook his head, her hair tickling his face with the movement. "He took me off all shows for a week." He fought the anger threatening to push through into his words as he walked her backward into her room. Or suite, rather. Two couches, a huge flat screen, and windows along the entire wall with a view of the Strip, lit up and sparkling on a wash of black night sky. "Are these the perks of being the girl the senior vice president of hotel operations is trying to win over?"

"Maybe the only one." She smiled, running her fingers through the hair at the back of his neck. "Listen, Declan, I'm really sorry about my dad. I feel responsible, and like I need to go talk to him—"

"I told you not to be sorry and I meant it." He gathered her long hair and pushed it to one side, revealing her long stretch of neck. "And you were not responsible. In fact, I'm grateful you never finished whatever assignment your mentor gave you, because if you had then you wouldn't have been at the beer garden tonight. And because you *were* there, I got to do this." He lowered his lips to hers and pressed a gentle kiss to them. "And this…" His fingers swept from her neck and traced an invisible line down the sides of her shirt. She closed her eyes and smiled, but too soon her eyes shot back open. Brows puckered.

"But maybe I should go back up there, try to convince him to let you do the shows?"

He lowered to the couch and pulled her down beside him. "Wouldn't do any good tonight. Right after you left, a security guard came and got him. Said there was an incident in the ballroom that needed his attention."

"The ballroom? That's where the ball was for the convention."

He didn't care about the convention or whatever happened there. He just wanted to drown himself in all things Melody so he could forget about the fact that he was going to be even farther behind with Brendan's money.

Declan hooked the tip of his finger into the strap of Melody's shirt and nudged her closer. "Come here." He pulled her to him, closing that space and inhaling her sweetness, then covered her mouth with his.

It was a slow kiss. A gentle kiss. One that filled him and emptied him at the same time. He was addicted to this mouth, to the feel of her skin against his, and this taste of her…

Was.

Not.

Fucking.

Enough.

He ran his hands from her shoulder down to her waist, and she must have had that exact thought because suddenly her hands were all over him and his on her, skimming the hem of her shirt. Through the thin material, his fingers found the dip of her belly button, the round underside of her tits. He groaned and slipped his hands beneath her shirt, pressing his palms flat along her smooth skin. Beside him she squirmed, letting out a low whimper. The sound was pure heroin—addicting and life changing—and he wound one hand around her waist and up her back to the clasp of her bra.

"This has to come off," he said, his lips against her neck. "Like, *now*." He fingered the clasp with one hand, his other hand still glued to her skin. The hooks didn't budge. He tried again. And again. Once more…

She giggled and nipped at his lip. "You need help?"

He shook his head, fighting a smile. "I've totally got this." Moving his fingers around in a different direction, he pinched the clasp, pulled the clasp, then let out a frustrated sigh. "Why do movies make this look so simple?" He leaned back and looked her straight in the eye, the smile winning. "One-handed bra removal is not easy. I call false reality."

"Teen boys all over the world are going to hate themselves for not being able to do it."

"Grown men, too."

"Don't forget Irish men." Melody readjusted herself and sat up straighter. "Declan?" she whispered, tipping her face toward his. Then she ran her tongue over his mouth and pinned his other hand against his side. "I don't want you to hate yourself. Don't give up. You've *got* this."

He laughed and dropped his face to her neck, still smiling. "We might be here until morning."

His hand worked the clasp, and after what seemed like a minute, he felt her breath feathering his ear. "Wow," she said with another giggle, "you are really bad at this. But I'll give you an A for effort." Her fingers brushed his away and unfastened the clasp with a simple flick of her wrists. Then she slid the straps down her arms and removed the bra, her shirt still on.

"Determination is one of my best qualities," he said with a smile, resting his palms along the span of skin between her collarbone and neckline. "But I'd be willing to fail at that too if I got to watch you do that again."

"Your botched attempt was actually quite sexy," she said, her muscles shivering as his hands settled over the thin straps of her tank top and stopped. Her breath hitched as seconds ticked past, her heart beating so loud he could hear it in the silence of the gigantic room.

He grinned. "So sexy I take your breath away?"

Her eyes met his, glossy and blown to the edges, and she shook her head. "You touching me does that…"

Declan felt his smile crinkle the edges of his eyes. "That wasn't a subtle hint."

She tipped her forehead to his, the bridge of her nose puckering. "I know."

"In fact, I think it was a complete failed attempt at one."

Her fingers ran over the hem of his shirt, dipping beneath the material directly above the button of his jeans. "I know."

"But I'll give you an A for effort." He'd give her an A for so many things: the beautiful gleam in her eyes, the delicate sound of her laugh, her ability to completely disarm him with only a simple touch.

Being with her was against his rule.

But being with her took away his pain.

They quietly stared at each other until he sank to her level and placed a long kiss against her lips. He peppered soft kisses all over her mouth until the kisses grew longer and more penetrating. His tongue finally swept across her lips to part them, and the playfulness died out.

Curling his finger underneath the straps, he dragged them down, freeing one breast and then the other. Silk caught briefly on her nipples, hardening them instantaneously. Gently he stripped her free of the shirt then stopped and studied every inch of her top half with a soundless intensity that was sure to unnerve her. Their breaths rose and fell together in an uneven, choppy rhythm. Heat pulsed and pounded in his boxers. Then he took her tits in his hands and growled.

"Christ, Melody. I want you." His mouth watered with the craving to taste her, to run his tongue under the line of her panties until she screamed against his mouth...

Instead, he flicked his tongue over her nipple, and her hips arched in his hands, as if she was desperate for release. Yeah, he could help her with that, just as soon as those jeans came off. She wiggled as he tugged, peeling the denim down to reveal her milky-smooth skin. Then he paused, studying the apex of her thighs. His hands rested on her hips, and he toyed with the lacy elastic band, running his thumb lightly along its edge. He grasped the fabric at both sides and began to work it down over her thighs, calves, then tore it away from her and tossed it to the floor.

She grinned up at him, goose bumps rising up on her legs as the cool air rushed over her skin. "Should I be worried that zero effort went into that?"

"That was all you, baby. A perfect ass makes for a perfect panty removal." His gaze scorched as he drank in the flesh revealed, anticipation cranking hard between them. He explored the crease at her thighs then traced an invisible line down the center of her body, watching every reaction in silence.

She sighed and whispered out, "Are you going to look at me all night or are you going to do something?"

Without an answer, he dipped his mouth and nipped at her earlobe, teased the tip of his tongue against the shell of her ear, then blew out a warm stream of breath. She jumped. He laughed and covered her lips with his, plunging his tongue into her mouth. She arched like a bow and clung to him, kissing him back.

But it wasn't enough. With her naked body scraping, pressing, grating against him, his patience was dwindling. Fast. Fingers itched to do much, much more. That warm, soft skin needed to be against his, and at the moment he had too many clothes on.

The same must've occurred to her, because her hands dipped beneath the hem of his shirt and scooted it up his chest. Next, she went for the button on his jeans, working madly until his legs were freed and the pants lay on the floor.

Declan's mouth moved to her breasts again, sucked her nipples as he stroked her belly and hips with his fingers, sliding lower and lower. He dipped one index finger along the folds of her wet clit to test her heat, drawing a slow groan from her. The sound nearly undid him, sending a hot wave of pure lust to the tip of his cock. The tip of his finger, too, as he plunged it inside her. Then another, rubbing delicately over the hard nub, just giving her a sample until—

Fuck, I have to taste her now.

He withdrew his hand and swiped the pad of his finger—glistening with her juices—across her bottom lip. Before she had a chance to react, he licked the trail then sucked her lip into his mouth.

"I'll die a happy man knowing I tasted that," he said, his lips lingering on hers.

Firmly, she clutched the sides of his head and said with an intense glint in her eye, "And I'll die a happy woman if you take another." To punctuate her words, she took his hand and wrapped those full lips around his finger.

Hot damn, she didn't have to say that twice.

With his other arm around her back, Declan stretched her out across the couch and settled between her legs. Her hips rolled forward as his hands grabbed her ass, a silent reassurance that this was definitely acceptable to her.

He lowered slowly, watching the anticipation play out on her face, lip caught between her teeth and eyes doe wide. That was, until his tongue licked her folds in a warm, wet stripe.

"Oh!"

Inside Declan smiled. She was like putty in his hands, and knowing he had that power spurred a beat of energy coursing throughout his entire body. And then he did it again, painfully slow, back to front, front to back, swirling his tongue over her clit until her eyes unfocused and her legs began to tremble.

Cramped on the tiny couch, his heartbeat was pulsing everywhere—his head, his ears, his throat, and...farther down south.

"Declan," Melody said, low and with an edge that pleaded for him to touch her. To do much, *much* more to her.

"I know." His words echoed in the room, sharp and biting, but the gentleness of the touch that followed—his fingers unfolding, sliding along her wet clit—drew out gasp after gasp from her.

She raised her hips into his hand, his mind telling his heart to slow the fuck down. He'd done this hundreds of times with who knew how many girls, and while Melody was by far one of the most beautiful, his hand shouldn't have been shaking at that very moment. He stroked her over and over until sweat glistened on her skin and his name tumbled off her lips.

Another swipe directly up the center, and her breath caught. "In," she blurted on an exhale, not blushing at all at what she was demanding. His tongue backtracked, retracing its path, and she sucked in another ragged breath. "Deep. Me. *Now.*"

Declan laughed, gliding the tip of one finger over her entrance. "Like this?" Her eyes started to roll back, and she reached for his hand as if she were desperate for him to jam the damn thing in when he snatched up her wrist and pinned her arm overhead. Leaning forward, he lowered his mouth to hers.

"F," she said against his lips with a slight growl. "You get an F because you are very slowly *killing* me."

He chuckled. "Hmm...in my book that would be an A plus plus." Then he descended at lightning speed, forcing their mouths together and sucking in her tongue just as his finger dived into her. With his other hand, he cupped her face, smoothing the back of his hand over her features, and watched his touch tip her over the edge.

She cried out, and her hips bucked as the climax took her hard. Her body shook with pleasure as he shed his boxers and covered himself with a condom. He slid back up her silken length, interlaced all ten fingers with hers, and pressed their joined hands into the couch cushions.

With his knee, he spread her legs wide open and took no time entering her. A thrust. A gasp. And man, did that make him smile. That was his favorite part—the catch of breath. How Melody's eyes widened at the very moment he penetrated into her delicious wetness. The most stunning woman he'd ever seen, so vulnerable to every touch.

Slowly at first, then increasing the speed, he pounded into her, his groans mingling with her whimpers. She moaned and pushed up her hips, her fingers digging into his hair as she held him against her and demanded him to dive deeper.

Then she looked up.

Wild hazel eyes filled with fire. Hunger. And a glaring request for more.

Hell, yeah, he could do more. With one hand he bound her wrists above her head and with the other he closed his fingers around her breast, the smooth skin a gratifying contrast to her taut nipple. She whimpered again and bowed upward for more. Inflamed for the taste of her, he lowered his head and sucked and bit until one of the tips was crimson red and gleaming. She panted and squirmed against the hold he had on her wrists.

"Let go of my hands," she demanded, a needy growl

following. "I want to touch you."

Shivers racked his body. He wanted her to touch him, too, but watching her face—a creation of erotic beauty—was something he surely couldn't miss.

He grinned and nipped at her lip. "Technically, you are touching me."

Another groan, this one filled with frustration. "With my hands. I want to feel you with my hands."

Very slowly, he traced a wet, hot line from her jaw to her ear and whispered, "I vaguely remember you once saying no touching allowed." And then he thrust into her again. Hard.

"Declan!" she screeched, her eyes crazed and almost panicked, like if she didn't put her hands on him in the next second she would shatter to pieces. The want he could see in her eyes—this want *for him*—was like a drug injected into his veins. It spurred him on, had him itching to claim more.

"Yes, Melody, show me how I please you. I want to see it all." He speared her with his eyes, drilling into her a promise to take everything she had. Then he sank all the way into her and held it, the tip of his cock pressed firmly against her sensitive spot.

Thrashing her head back and forth, she cried out, "More, give me more."

"Come for me, Melody." With a gentle ease, he retreated and thrust again, holding his erection to her inside walls, longer this time.

"Oh, God—I can't—I'm going to—"

He bit her nipple as he withdrew and charged one last time, her nails digging punishingly into his knuckles. A scream ripped through the air as she shuddered and arched against him, and he held her as he drew out her orgasm, keeping her body pressed to his. He'd known they had chemistry between them, but nothing prepared him for the surge of emotion that hit his gut full force when she sighed out his name. He wanted to fall asleep every night to that sound. Wake up every morning to it. Jesus, where had such tender thoughts come from?

After a moment and a long exhale, Melody grew limp. Then she giggled. "Can I have my hands back now? I'd like to return the favor."

Favor? Was that what she thought this was? Another bout of mindless sex to erase a horrible day?

Was it?

Suddenly he didn't know. Sexual chemistry aside, there was something heavier—a connection growing between them.

Releasing her hands, he narrowed his stare on her. "If that's all it's going to be—a *favor*—then I don't want it."

Her eyes searched his, and damn that connection. It was like she was reaching in and scraping the insides of his chest. "It's not," she said, her head drooping and pink staining her cheeks. "I mean…it wasn't for me."

The tip of his finger tilted her chin up, his eyes meeting hers again. "Good." Softly, his knuckles swiped along her skin. "Just so we're clear on that." Then he lifted her, flinging his back to the couch and dropping her on top of him, her legs straddled across his midsection.

A silent moment passed, her fingertips dragging up and down his stomach. The sight—a gorgeous blond-haired beauty silhouetted against the ceiling lights—was something out of a dream.

Slowly she shifted. Then slid her wet folds over his hardened cock and rode him into oblivion.

Chapter Seven

A soft tingly touch ran up Melody's bare arm. Mother of everything holy, would she ever be able to move on from the way Declan made her feel? She'd be going home in the morning, which meant this would be the last time she'd ever see him, and for some reason that thought felt like a pile of books on her chest, sinking her farther into the fluffy couch of her hotel room.

A phone appeared in front of her, a colorful keyboard on the screen. She looked to Declan, and he smiled. "It's a music app to learn to play piano. Full-size eighty-eight keyboard, integrated metronome, sophisticated learning mode…" He trailed off as he caught her staring at him, bemused. He plopped the phone into her hand and shrugged. "I figured you'd want something at home, and I'm guessing you don't have a piano where you live." He tapped the phone screen a few times and a song started to play—Hozier's "Take Me to Church." "Or you can just watch the computer play and imagine it's me."

Oh, she'd be imagining him all right. But likely in her bed at night, not while staring at a phone.

"Care if I get a drink?" he asked, dropping a kiss onto her cheek then hopping off the couch to find his pants.

She held out his phone and attempted to pry her sated body from where they'd been lying since that amazing round of sex. Sex that wasn't just hot like the first time, but jarring on a whole other level. Because she'd felt something when he'd said he didn't want a favor. Something that satisfied her in a completely different way. Her soul. It was like he'd touched her soul.

Smiling up at him, she said, "I'll get it. What would you like?"

With a hand cradled around her neck, he took her in a bruising kiss. Sweeping his tongue once, twice. Then he spun and sauntered to the minibar, where he searched out a glass, a small bottle of Jameson, and a ginger ale. For a moment, she just watched his backside, the muscles in his shoulders pinching and bunching with the movement. Fascinated by the beauty of it. Yeah, it might be a long time before she ever forgot *that* sight—

A buzz of the phone broke her daze. A text from someone named Nurse Lewis. Why would a nurse be texting Declan? A hot jolt of jealousy burned through her. Another fling? A Declan groupie he'd met at Napoleon's?

Her skin bristled all the way to her fingertips and, without thinking, she clicked on the message.

Brendan's functioning nerves are failing, which means we need to reroute faster. Surgery needs to be *this month. Will you have the $ by then?*

Brendan... Melody recognized that name as Declan's brother. He'd said his brother was back in Ireland. That he hadn't seen him in a while.

"Um..." Melody cleared her throat, unsure of the next words to say. She had no idea what the message meant, but talk of surgery and failing nerves and needing money—

Money. Was that why he was desperate for her to talk to her father?

Declan held up an extra glass. "You want one, too? There's plenty."

She shook her head and twisted the phone his way. "Someone texted you. Nurse Lewis? She said...um... Well, maybe you should read it."

In just a few steps he was across the room, the phone in his hands, his eyes scanning and then squinting at the screen. A tic formed at his jaw with the clench of it. Livid, this message—whatever it meant—set him on fire.

Melody peeled herself off the couch and approached him. "I didn't mean to pry."

Silence.

She tried again, resting her hand on his tensed arm. "Your brother... Is he sick? Why does he need surgery?"

His fingers were already tapping a return message. Once he was done, he looked down at her, pain and anguish twisting his features. His lips mashed together, and for a fleeting moment Melody thought he was going to shut down, not talk to her at all and leave. Instead, he tucked his phone into his pocket and faced her. "Quadriplegic. He was in an accident a few months ago that took away his ability to move.

There's a surgery that supposedly can give him back the use of his limbs—which means play the guitar again—but it's going to cost a fortune."

"How much?"

"Tens of thousands. Depends on how bad the nerves are once doctors get in there to reroute them. And according to his nurse, every day that goes by, more nerves fail and that price goes up." The somberness of his voice was like a fissure forming inside her. It hurt her to see him this way. And what hurt her even more?

The coin jar with a B on it, the look on his face when he'd told her he'd been taken off shows for a week. The desperate plea to help him obtain the higher-paying slot the first night they'd met...Melody could have seen it if she hadn't been so wrapped up in her own problems.

Standing there in the middle of her spacious, lavish hotel room, she suddenly had an idea. "Let's talk to my father in the morning. I know he was upset about what happened tonight, but he's not heartless. If we tell him about your brother, I'm sure we can convince him to give you the Parrot Lounge slot."

"What do you think?"

Melody's father sat back in his recliner and threw his gaze up to the whirring ceiling fan. He inhaled through his nose, letting the flood of explanation about Declan's brother and their need for money—on top of Declan being the optimal choice for the Parrot Lounge—sink in.

"Sounds to me," he finally said, crossing his arms over

his midsection, his features set firmly on his face, "like you're stepping into a managerial position. The problem with that is you're…not. A manager. Yet, anyway."

She shook her head. "Dad, no. I don't want to be a manager. Ever. I just want to help out a friend." At that word— *friend*—Melody's chin twitched with the urge to turn to the doorway, where Declan awaited outside.

Her father's eyebrow rose, likely recalling what he had walked in on last night. The way she'd been sucking face with one of his employees. The same employee he, in his eyes, had introduced her to only the day before. "Is that how you treat all of your *friends*?"

Her cheeks flushed at his words, but she sat up straighter, pushing her back into the chair. "I'm a grown adult, Dad. Please don't lecture me on petty high school stuff. Declan was teaching me how to play piano and we—"

"Piano?" Another brow lift.

Nodding, Melody shifted across from him. Explaining music therapy wasn't why she'd come here, to her father's office, and would only throw this conversation off track. "Never mind. Declan needs our help. Besides, we both know he can draw the crowds, and you said yourself he was really talented. Why *wouldn't* you put him at the Parrot Lounge?"

Her father studied her, his narrow-set eyes crawling over her face. "We also know he's really good at pissing off my customers. I don't need that kind of behavior in my hotel, especially at my top-selling bar."

Something blossomed inside Melody's chest, snaking out to her shoulders and down to her ribs. Anger? Frustration? She just wanted her dad to see the same gentle, caring side she had seen in Declan. The way he didn't brush off the fact that she had a reading disability but found something online that could help her overcome it.

Melody drew in a deep breath and gripped the sides of her chair. "I think the money he could make you at the Parrot far outweighs the few mistakes he's made. You want more sales? More customers? More talk about how fabulous your hotel is? Declan can do that for you."

Her father snatched a pen from the desk and tapped it along the wood. A long moment passed, then he speared her with a challenging look. "Why don't you hire him for the Parrot?"

Melody blinked. "Me? How? I don't work for the ho—"
Oh.

"Mel, you have the power to make any decision you want at the Masquerade. Head manager? You have to admit, it rings a nice little bell."

Head manager?

What?

No. Melody's hands shot up to stop her father's wasted words. "It's not what I want." Or was it what she was scared of? Suddenly it was like she'd been dunked into a vat of molten-hot doubt.

Her insides clenched, her conversation with Declan about what she wanted replaying in her mind. *You're scaring yourself into not believing in yourself.*

Sitting in the spacious office, surrounded by large, framed photos of the hotel's extravagant water feature outside, Declan's words, her father's words, and her words scrambled together like the colors of a child's finger paint-ing. They made sense. They didn't make sense. And all this muddled confusion dizzied her.

"What you want is a promotion for your *friend*," her father said, sounding more like he was spitting out the words than speaking them. "And this is the only way I'm going to give it to you. In fact, I'm thinking I might permanently replace him with Riley Banks. Riley can draw pretty decent crowds, too, you know…"

"You're going to fire Declan?" Melody shot to her feet, a sickening panic welling in her belly. Declan was already struggling to earn the money for his brother's surgery. What would he do if he didn't have a job at all? She looked down at her father—at his reclined feet and tightened expression. "Are you crazy? You can't toy with someone's life like that!"

"I'm your father, and I know what's best for you."

"What's best for me is to not be blackmailed into taking over a hotel by ruining someone else's life! I can't believe you right now."

What scared her the most was that she knew her father, knew how stubborn he was. If he had it in his head that he wanted her to become head manager of the hotel, she had no doubt that he would do something drastic to get his way.

Like fire Declan.

Her stomach fell to her toes.

How would she live with herself if he lost his job because of her?

Her father lifted the pen to his mouth, paused, then looked up at Melody. "I've got some business to take care of. What time are you leaving today? Let's have lunch before you go."

She stepped toward the door. So many words fought to come out of her mouth. She wanted to yell at him for using Declan to get what he wanted. Scream at him to stop treating her like he knew what was best for her, when there was no way he could possibly have any idea what it was like to be her. Words twisted and tangled and knotted until eventually they sat as a heavy lump at the base of her throat.

Without a word, she walked out and the door slammed behind her. She looked to Declan, sitting on the hallway bench, anticipation and optimism blasting through his gaze. How in the world was she going to break the news to him?

He stood when he saw her, and at the same time her father's office door flew open. "Mel—"

Her father stopped, eyes locked on Declan. He licked his lips. "Mr. Waterford," he said, his gaze skipping back and forth between Declan and her. "Perfect timing. I'd like to speak to you in my office."

Oh, no…

Declan straightened his stance, standing tall, smiled and nodded.

Smiled. *Double oh, no!* "Declan," she blurted out, reaching for his arm, "I don't think—"

His smile grew, stretched from ear to ear. He patted her hand and whispered, "Thank you."

"No." She tried to step in front of him, but he was already skating toward the door. "It's not what you—"

He's not going to give you the job!

Declan crossed the threshold. Her father mouthed something that looked like the word "manager" and then the door shut.

Oh my God, oh my God, oh my God. What was she supposed to do? Leave? Stay? Bang on the stupid door?

Her body felt like it was on fire, her heart exploding from the inside out. Breaking for Declan and his brother.

As much as she was trying to convince herself that it meant nothing, she knew it did. Every minute they were together, she fell a little harder for him. Whether it was the gentle smile he offered when she was hurting on the inside or the way he made her laugh, more and more pieces of her heart were becoming his.

Five minutes passed.

Ten.

Several people sauntered past with a security escort, laughing and looking like they were still dressed from last night's ball. "That poor ass. It was so red," one of them said—a girl about her age, brown hair pulled into a twist and red satin sashaying against the heels she dangled from her fingers.

"Maybe the gift shop will start carrying assless chaps," her friend responded and they both burst out laughing. A pang of sadness clung to Melody's chest. If she wasn't an intern, she would've gone to that ball and avoided this entire mess from last night—the misunderstanding with Karri, the interrupted kiss by her father…all of it.

Across the hall, a *click* sounded, and then the door opened.

Declan gripped the door so hard, he was sure he was leaving finger indentations in the wood, considering every single part of him, straight down to his shoes, had just clenched as he spotted Melody. Simply standing there. Watching him.

Mr. Sumner's words echoed through his head like it was

a goddamn concert hall. *Refusing to follow policy. Inappropriate conduct on hotel grounds. Engaging in confrontation with a customer. Property damage.* Was there anything he didn't fucking do?

The last was the worst, though. Those words—*you're fired*—drilled a hole as deep as the Grand Canyon into his chest. He peeked over his shoulder at the man who had just completely destroyed everything he had been working for. Mr. Sumner lifted the phone to his ear. Tapped his fingers along the keyboard. What a motherfucking spanner.

From the bench where she'd been waiting, Melody rushed over to him, her arms extended. His mind screamed at him to block her, to bat away her hands and not allow any contact whatsoever. Obviously his body had a different idea, reaching out to her, pulling her into him. Damn the softness of her skin and the sweet smell he would never be able to get out of his memory. His body craved the feel of her. Craved it hard, like a damn addiction. "Don't," he eventually managed to spit out, gritting against the ache growing in his jaw.

She eased back and looked into his eyes. "Did he fire you?"

The temperature inside him kicked up a hundred degrees. Why did it feel like he was melting from the inside out? "You knew he was going to? Why didn't you talk to him? Convince him not to?"

No money. No money. No money.

Melody paused, her mouth working side to side to form words. And that was all the answer he needed. She hadn't tried to stop it. Stop *him*. Her father.

No surgery. No surgery. No surgery.

Declan pushed back, leaving a widening space between

them. Melody's features pinched. "I tried," she whispered. "But it's…it's complicated."

Complicated? Was she kidding? "Apparently I've missed something, because asking your father not to fire someone shouldn't be complicated at all."

"I did ask him, but…" Her arms wrapped around her middle. "He doesn't just want me to manage the hotel, he wants me to take over the whole thing. Become the head manager."

"And…" His arms flung out to the sides, yet another sign he was losing his patience. If he didn't walk out soon, there would be a pretty good chance he would be leaving a fist-sized hole in the fucking wall.

Melody glanced up at him, her expression full of everything and nothing at the same time. "And if I do," she said, her voice weaker than before, "then I can rehire you…into the top slot at the Parrot."

He knew just by the sound of her voice, she wasn't going to take the position. Still, he had to ask. "Please tell me you're planning on accepting his offer."

She shook her head, a sea of blond curtaining her face. "I can't…"

Had he actually thought a stranger he'd met only a few days ago would?

If he was honest with himself, yes. Because she didn't feel like a stranger. She didn't feel like someone he'd only met seventy-two hours ago. The connection they had was penetrating and invasive and something he'd never felt with any other woman, and that had to mean something. Didn't it?

Obviously it didn't mean jack to her. And that hope that

had been swelling in his chest like an extra lung was now choking him. No money. No surgery. The ceiling suddenly felt as if it was collapsing on him.

He sucked in a breath through his nose. Maybe she really had just been using him for music lessons. Maybe he should've stuck to using her for her connections instead of letting his heart get in the way. Maybe then he would still have a goddamn job.

That last thought hit him full force. He didn't have a job. No money, no surgery. *I'm so sorry, Brendan.*

Declan pushed past Melody, holding his breath so he wouldn't smell the very scent that had driven him crazy only a few hours ago. "I guess I better hit the streets then. I hear job hunting in Vegas is a bitch."

A warm hand grabbed his wrist. "Declan, wait. You don't have to do this alone—raise the money for your brother."

"Really?" He scowled, taking another step backward. "Because my parents are gone and there's no other family. His former bandmates despise the both of us because their chance at going big is now shot, so who else is there?"

"Me...I can help you."

The room tilted. "You?" he scoffed. *Right.* He yanked his arm from her grasp and spouted over his shoulder as he marched down the hallway and toward the elevator, "I think you've helped enough."

Silence—the kind that sank into his bones—followed his footsteps. With every scuff of his shoe, every beat of his heart, every lungful of air pushed out, that silence became heavier and heavier. Until it was screaming in his ears.

A new job—that was now his priority, and he swore to himself and on his brother's recovery that he wasn't going to sleep until he found one.

"So you're the only one," Melody called out from behind him, sounding close enough that she must've been following him. "That doesn't mean you have to beat yourself up over this."

Hands, it felt like hands had reached up from the carpet and grabbed onto his legs. And then they were whirling him around, fast and hard. "What else would you expect the person who caused the accident to do?"

He'd never said those words out loud before. They sounded wrong, like their edges were catching on his lips.

Melody blinked. "Caused?"

Declan gritted his teeth, more foreign words threatening to escape. They pushed at his lips, pulled at his tongue. He wanted to tell her. He didn't.

Another breath, then he closed his eyes. "I'm the one who told Brendan to jump first. I told him the water was deep enough even though I hadn't checked. And I'm the one who sat in the hospital room and watched his face as the doctors told him he would never walk or use his arms again. *That's* why I'm beating myself up over this. Because I have to. Because if I don't, then who will? I refuse to let my brother be alone."

The elevator was only a few steps away. He could feel the doors at his back. He reached behind and pushed the down button. Melody stood in the middle of the hallway, her arms dangling loosely at her sides, the corners of her mouth pulling into a frown and tears brimming in her eyes.

"I didn't know..."

The elevator *dinged*, and the doors slid open. "Now you do..." Then he stepped into the elevators, looking anywhere but at Melody until the doors closed.

The drive home was a blur, Declan's mind racing over his brother and surgery and how the hell he was going to earn the money now as he wove through the Strip's traffic. The weight of being unemployed, of telling his brother...

He'd thought for sure that by coming to Vegas he was going to be able to fix his brother, repay the immeasurable debt to him. Instead, he'd ruined everything. Trusting Melody to talk to her father had been a mistake. Allowing himself to feel anything for her had been, too. Because what did he have to show for it?

So engulfed in the flood of worry, he didn't see the blue minivan pulling out of space forty-three of his apartment's parking lot until his front fender was smashed against the van's rear end.

"Godmotherfuckingdammit!" he shouted, slamming his palm into the steering wheel. From where he was sitting, he could see Ms. Johnson's van would need a new back fender. He wasn't about to tell his insurance company that. Which meant the money he'd earned thus far would be paying for it.

He threw his head back against the headrest and closed his eyes. *Fuck. My. Life.*

Chapter Eight

She could still smell him. At the door. On the couch. Near the bar. She could feel him, too. Everywhere. Declan was everywhere in her hotel room, and everything in her room was Declan. It made her wonder if Declan felt her, too, but the thought slipped away just as fast as it came.

He hadn't told her good-bye, but she knew by the way he wouldn't look at her as the elevator doors had swallowed him up that the chance was as slim as hitting the jackpot that he would be showing up at her room before she had to leave in an hour. She inhaled a deep breath, an attempt to relieve the growing pressure in her chest. He hadn't said good-bye, but she knew it was. She was leaving for California and, since her father was into toying with people's lives, Declan would no longer have a reason to be at the Masquerade.

Her purse landed with a *thunk* on the small table separating the two couches, and her eyes couldn't help but scan the smooth white leather, the memory of her skin sliding and pressing into the cool material, with Declan's hands as a deliciously warm contrast. His mouth on hers, him inside her—

You came back to pack, not ogle a couch, dummy. Stay focused.

But first she had to call Karri. Every muscle in her body sagged. The editorial letter to Justine, one of the company's newest authors, needed to be finished and sent this morning. If she didn't have the letter, then she couldn't start her edits, and then the book wouldn't have a chance at making its scheduled December release.

One drink. She was supposed to go out and have one drink with Heather then come back and work on the letter. Instead, she'd gotten sucked into the world of Declan. It was like looking through a telescope when she was with him—he was the only thing she could see.

Was that normal? Was that what being attracted to someone was like?

She knew by the crack growing in her heart that over the last few days, she'd grown more than simply attracted to Declan Waterford. She'd fallen for him. Felt things with him that she'd never felt before.

Her eyes fell on the wide door to the outside hallway, willing him to knock on it. For him to show up and scoop her into his arms and hold her, telling her… What could he possibly tell her? That he wanted to come to California with her? Yeah, that wouldn't happen. That she should stay in Vegas? Take the house her father had purchased? That *definitely* wouldn't happen.

It was like her blood turned to sludge, pushing slowly and heavily through her veins. There wasn't a reason for her to see Declan again, which meant she wasn't going to. She closed her eyes and allowed herself one millisecond to commit everything about him to memory—his deep green eyes, the way his mouth quirked up more on the left side than the right when he smiled, the sense of calm that being in his arms provided.

One millisecond to entomb *him*, and then she picked up the phone and dialed Karri's number. Three long rings— enough time for that nervous edge she always got when talking with her boss to prickle at the back of her neck, topped off with the dread of hearing the words she knew would likely be coming—*after last night I don't think we can continue this internship*—then Karri's voice was in her ear, sounding slower and groggier than she normally did.

"I owe you an apology."

Wait. *What?*

"I think it's the other way around," Melody said. "I'm sorry I didn't finish the letter."

Something rustled against the phone, and her boss cleared her throat. "We'll talk about that in a minute, but regardless if you finished or not, I shouldn't ever have said your work would be crap."

Oh, she remembered that? A flush shot into Melody's cheeks. If Karri remembered what she'd said, then she likely remembered the way she had been wrapped around Declan and what had happened after, too. Declan's words. Security.

The rustling sounded again—blankets, maybe?—and Karri continued. "Listen, I may have had a little too much to drink last night, and I may have said some things to you I'm not proud of—which I'm sorry about—but I also need to know that you are in this internship 200 percent."

"I am," Melody said quickly. "I promise you—"

"I'm not finished." Karri interrupted in her firm, yet scratchier-than-normal voice. "One thing you need to understand is obtaining the internship is easy. Lots of editors train lots of interns, but very few are actually offered a position in the company. Competition for those positions is fierce, and only those who go above and beyond stand out enough to even be considered for them. I need to see that you are willing to make sacrifices, including spending the evening with an extremely hot guy, if you want a glowing recommendation from me at the end of this." A pause, but only long enough for Karri's words to barely trickle in. "Let me ask you this. Is working in publishing what you really want?"

What she wanted…

All her life, working in this business was all she'd wanted, up until the moment Declan told her she was scared of what she thought she couldn't do. Working in the hotel was what he'd been talking about, but…that fear drenched her like a bucket of cold water when she was working for Karri, too. Would she do everything right? Was there someone who could do it better? Was she even good enough?

The sun exploded in bright yellow radiance through the hotel window, stabbing golden rays across the carpet. A shallow breath filled her lungs, and then she answered Karri.

"Yes…" Her boss had asked if she wanted this job, not if she thought she would be good at it. Totally different in Melody's mind.

Karri chuckled. "You're not very convincing, if you ask me."

Crap. It was, and she needed Karri to know it was. Either

that or the next words out of Karri's mouth were going to be *it was nice knowing you, Melody Sumner.*

"You're at that age where you're struggling with what you want to do with your life. I get that," Karri said. "Believe it or not, I was there once, too." Her boss laughed, as if what she'd said was a joke. Melody stood frozen, the carpet scraping at the edges of her feet. *Please don't say you're letting me go. Don't say it, don't say it, don't say it.* "I want you to take a few days to think about what you want. *Really* think about it. And then we'll talk about where to go from here."

She wasn't being let go. But she wasn't continuing, either. She was…being put on hold? What did that even mean?

"Okay," Melody responded, because what else was she supposed to say to that? She lowered herself onto the couch and sagged into the cushions.

Karri ended the call with, "Talk to you in a few days then," and Melody slammed her eyes shut. *I need to convince Karri this is what I want.* But inside, her mind was screaming the one question Declan had laid on her last night.

What is it you really want?

D eclan's fingers skimmed his keyboard, the sun glaring off the shiny white ivory. When was the last time he'd played outside? Or this keyboard at all? It'd been tucked away in his closet since moving to the States, a gift from Brendan after he'd been unable to play it.

Ironic… Once his brother's, and now he was using it as a means to earn money *for* his brother. And on a street corner in Vegas? In front of the very hotel he used to perform at?

With a crumpled ball of useless classifieds next to him? Pathetic.

But he was desperate. Only a few days had passed since he'd been fired from the Masquerade, but one thing was clear—finding another gig out here in Vegas *was* going to be a bitch.

Street corners were for homeless people. And those douche bags handing out titty flyers. Apparently, they were for losers who couldn't hold a hotel gig, too. He deserved to be here—punishment for failing his brother and the powerless way it made him feel.

His fingers started in on the opening strains of Ellie Goulding's "Love Me Like You Do." The song brought in great tips in Nap's. Maybe it would here, too, with the glut of tourists looking to experience Vegas.

A few coins clunked against the red felt of his keyboard case. A few dollar bills floated in as well. At this rate, he'd have to play for five years before he had enough to fix Brendan. The weight on his chest grew heavier. What was he doing? He'd make more money standing on a street corner with a sign that said ANYTHING HELPS.

As the last verse of the song mumbled off his lips, his phone rang with Brendan's ringtone—a song the band had written and recorded only a few weeks before the accident. While fans would never know based on the lyrics about a boat making it through a storm, Declan knew that song was the band's way of acknowledging they were on their way up in the world of indie rock.

If they'd written that song after the accident, the damn boat would've sunk, just like their band. Just like Brendan's hope of becoming a star and Declan's fucking ability to make it up to his brother.

He lifted the phone to his ear and answered the call.

"You know," his brother said, sounding cheerful as ever, "I feel like I've forgotten what your ugly face looks like." Declan smiled. Some things, regardless of what had happened, never changed.

"Lucky for you, you're going to be staring at it every damn day in about a week." Just as soon as he earned enough to afford the plane ticket back to Ireland. He had no idea what he was going to do for money once he was there, but at least he'd be able to help his brother out in the meantime. He'd be his brother's goddamn servant if that was what he wanted.

"What is that supposed to mean?" Brendan asked, the exuberance morphing into something…less exuberant.

Declan sighed and kicked shut the keyboard case with the tip of his shoe. "Lost my job here, brother, and no other hotels are looking for performers right now. That means I'm coming home to spoon-feed your ass and wipe it when it comes out the other end."

"Bullshit you are. Currently, I have a sexy-as-hell nurse doing that, and I'll be damned if it's your face I have to see every morning instead of hers. Besides…" Brendan paused, sucking in an audible breath—a noise Declan still hadn't grown used to. "Haven't you met anyone yet? Surely Vegas is crawling with big tits and beautiful smiles."

Yeah, it was. Especially one who didn't belong here at all. He hadn't seen Melody since he'd left her standing in the hallway near her father's office, but from the hollowness spreading through his chest each day that passed, a piece of his heart seemed to stay with her that day. But how did he tell his brother that? He'd found someone who took his mind off *him*? Off the relentless and unforgiving guilt he'd felt since the moment they'd heard doctors spout Brendan's fate?

Never going to happen. His job was to fix Brendan; nothing else mattered until then.

But that hollowness in his chest felt as if it had life, and as he sat on the stool watching people stroll by, it mutated into a fog of remorse that clung to his very bones. He never should have treated Melody the way he had—blaming her for what her father had done. Making her feel as if she should've accepted her father's offer to become manager just to help him out. "Ass" wasn't even close to what he'd been to her—

"Earth to the broody mothereffer on the line," his brother said with a wheezing laugh. "I'm going to take your uncharacteristic silence as confirmation on that one. What's her name and when do I get to meet her?"

Declan chuckled halfheartedly. "I may have met someone. Melody," he admitted, staring down at his keyboard. Rays from the early afternoon sun glinted off the glossy keys, stabbing him in the eyes. He welcomed the pain. "She's not from here, though. And she left a few days ago. Plus, I was an asshole to her, so seeing her—or even dreaming of it—would be a waste of my time." Not to mention the fact that since coming to the States, Declan had sworn off women completely, and if he wanted to focus on how to get his brother this surgery he probably should go back to that. Melody had broken through his walls, and he wasn't sure how it had happened in such a short time.

You know exactly why, dipshit.

Her smile. Her laugh. The way her eyes would narrow and lips would twitch when she was holding back something crude. The time they'd shared was more than piano teacher and student. More than performer looking for a promotion. It was a connection—one he'd never experienced with a woman before.

"By the woe-is-me sound to your voice," Brendan said, "she sounds like someone worth going after." Brendan was older than him, someone he'd always looked up to. But the nonsense he was saying needed to stop.

Declan shook his head. "Not an option, B. We need to get you this surgery, which means the only thing I'm doing right now is figuring out how to pay for it."

"It's not your problem, and you need to stop acting as if it is."

"Not my problem?" Declan rolled his shoulders back and smiled politely at the cluster of twenty-something girls flashing their *what happens in Vegas stays in Vegas* grins. "Everything about it is my problem. *You* are my brother. *I* made you jump—"

"You never made me jump."

"Don't cut me off, dick. I was saying I made you jump *first*."

"Is that what this is about? That I'm sitting in this chair instead of you?"

Yes. "Yes." It's what it had always been about. "I lied to you and told you it was safe to jump. If I hadn't been so caught up in myself and gone down to check the depth, you would be on top of the world with the band and I never would've had reason to come to this shithole of a town."

He never would've met Melody, either. Quickly he

shook that thought away.

"You're blaming yourself…" No judgment in his brother's voice. Just an out-loud realization. And what could Declan say to that? Not like it was new information to him. He blamed himself. He always would. At least until Brendan was fixed.

Silence filled the line, the chatter and scuffling sounds of people walking past, flitting in and out of it like a buzzing fly in his ear. Ten seconds. Twenty. And then Brendan continued.

"You're not coming back here."

"Like hell I'm not."

"Listen to me, Dec. You weren't the only one drinking that day, and you definitely weren't the only one set on jumping. What happened was an accident, one that could've happened to anyone."

"But it happened to you."

"Which I'm fine with."

Suddenly it was hard to breathe, like four invisible walls were pressing in on him. "Are you fine that you lost your band because of it, too?" Declan snapped. "That was your dream, and now it's gone. Don't tell me you're okay with that."

"I wasn't at first."

"But you are now?" How could he be okay with it? He'd lost everything. *Everything.* Declan's insides curled in on him. Those walls closing in faster and faster, stealing all the air. "How?" The last word only a whisper, even though his mind was screaming it.

"Remember how Grams always talked about presidents?"

Declan laughed. How could he not? It was *all* she talked about. "Yeah."

"Well, a few months before she died, she was talking to me about the band. I didn't want to leave her to record the album, but she was insisting that I go. She said if there was one thing she had learned in her lifetime it was that in the end it wasn't the years in your life, but the life in your years. Some quote by Abraham Lincoln. She wanted me to go to give my years life."

Declan ran a hand over his face. "Which is exactly why you need this surgery. To put the life back in *this* year, and every one after." Not be stuck in a wheelchair, depending on everyone else to do things for him.

"The surgery isn't the issue, Dec. We'll get the surgery. I've applied for a couple of grants, and my nurse has even set up an online fund. I'm talking about you taking on the burden of feeling like it's solely your responsibility. It's not, and it never will be, and I refuse to be the reason you come home. You want to come back here, then fine, but you will not do it because of me."

The words were coming at him too fast to process. Grant? Fund? Get the surgery?

"There's a time stamp on that surgery," Declan spouted, his mind twisting and turning like a fucked-up roller coaster.

"And I've got it handled, brother. Don't forget that I'm still older and smarter than your pretty-boy ass. Now stop worrying about me and go track down that chick of yours."

Declan focused on his fingers, his thumb that was resting on middle C. *Melody Sumner, meet middle C.* How was it that someone could blast into his life with such magnitude and life-altering force? Could penetrate his walls and infiltrate his soul?

He said "'bye" and ended the call with his brother. The

brother who didn't need him. Or his help. Didn't want him going back home, either. He had no job, no real reason to stay in Vegas, and as all of those realizations slammed into him one by one, each one harder and harder, it left him feeling like a kid lost in a store. Empty and alone.

And then there was Melody. The beautiful woman he'd been an ass to. The one he'd walked away from. She never deserved to be treated the way he had, and he felt like the world's biggest spanner for not at the very least calling her to apologize.

Sitting in the warm sunlight, his eyes fell to the crumpled ball of classifieds near his case. *Nothing holding you in Vegas, Waterford.* Six simple words, but the weight of them and the idea that sprouted along with them had him off his stool and packing up his keyboard in seconds.

If Brendan didn't need help fixing himself, then there was something else he needed to fix.

Chapter Nine

Mail in one hand, groceries in her other, Melody shuffled up the flower-lined walkway to the front door of her two-story townhome. It wasn't the nicest or grandest complex in town, but the cute shutters and upper-floor balcony had drawn her in. The vibe there was quiet and quaint, and just the way she liked it.

At the door, she fumbled with her keys, noticing from the corner of her eye that the SOLD sign next door had finally come down. Blinds covered the one large window beside the door and a small stack of boxes sat at the doorstep. She hadn't met the new owners yet, but whoever it was, she thought as she jiggled the lock loose and swung open her door, had to be better than the witch lady who'd lived there before. Witch Lady wasn't friendly, never smiled, and had cats that pooped all over her front doorstep. Melody didn't know what had happened to her—she'd been gone when she returned from the Romance Lovers Convention a few weeks ago. She didn't much care, either. *Good riddance.*

Inside her living room, the sweet, floral scent hit her before the large vase of brilliantly colored flowers came into view. Flowers that had arrived a few days ago. Flowers that, at first, she'd thought were from Declan—a truce on his part for the way he had acted the day she left. But they were from her father, an apology for trying to push her into something she didn't want. They'd had a few conversations since she'd been home, she and her father, mostly discussing how she saw her future. Turned out her dad had just been worried that the editorial internship wouldn't be enough, wouldn't lead to a full-time job she'd be able to support herself on.

Also turned out that Declan had been right about one thing. She *was* holding back and was scared of what she couldn't do. But managing the hotel, Melody realized, wasn't what she was avoiding. It was the internship. The possibility of working the rest of her life in a job she felt incapable of doing at times. The mistakes, the struggles... It was as if her subconscious was telling her all along that she would never make it with only one toe in.

So she held her breath and jumped.

No, cannonballed. Straight into the deepest waters of the job. Over the past few weeks, she'd put everything she had into her work. Reading manuscripts, drafting letters, contacting authors and agents. And over those past few weeks, one thing became clear. She was actually quite good at her job. Even Karri had noticed and had discussed the possibility of hiring Melody as her assistant.

Assistant editor.

It wasn't where she wanted to be in the end, but it was a start.

Melody dropped her mail and groceries onto the counter then slipped out of her shoes and settled on the couch to finish reading the manuscript she'd started the day before.

The ringing of the doorbell woke her and Melody popped off the couch as if she hadn't accidentally fallen asleep while reading. Jumping in all the way didn't mean she didn't still struggle with the words. Even with the online piano lessons she'd been completing, her mind still scrambled words into a dizzying cyclone. The lessons, however, were simply helping her manage the confusion better.

She padded to the door and tugged it open with a smile, knowing there was a good chance this could be her first meeting with her new neighbors.

Bright sun filled the...empty doorstep? Huh? She glanced from side to side and even down the walkway toward the parking lot. Then at her feet, something shiny caught her attention. A metal tin with a lid, much like one takeout food would come in.

Carefully, she crouched down, her eyes still scanning the grassy yards past hers, and sniffed. Tomatoes, basil, cheese — something Italian. Lasagna? Across the way, the window facing her was now unshrouded with blinds. Beyond the glass, a solid figure moved past. A man, by the broad shoulders and muscled chest. But that was all she could see.

She lifted the lid on the tin. Sure enough, it was lasagna. *What an odd gift from a neighbor.*

And shouldn't it have been the other way around — her bringing something to the people new to her neighborhood?

Tucking her fingers beneath it, she lifted the warm container then stood. As the door was about to shut, someone called out, "Do you mind sharing?"

Melody froze. That voice. It was deep and sexy and very, very familiar.

Declan.

But how? He didn't know where she lived—didn't even know what city. Besides, he lived in Vegas. And would have no reason to come to her small town in California...

Pulling the door open a sliver, she peeked out.

Declan grinned. Melody looked just as surprised as he'd expected, with her eyes round as golf balls and her lips parted into a *What the fuck are you doing here?* gape. Mentally, he snapped a picture—it was more priceless than he could've imagined—then pointed to the tin in her grasp.

"I'm new to the neighborhood," he said, pausing another moment to let those words sink in. One breath. Two. Then her gaze flickered over his shoulder at his new front door then back to him. When he'd found out where Melody lived, moving in next to her hadn't even crossed his mind. Find her, apologize, ask for her forgiveness was what he'd planned. But the tiny town filled with lush trees and red dirt had reminded him of home, but not. Made him miss his brother, but also remember what Brendan had told him—that he should *find his chick*.

However, Melody was no chick. She was smart and funny and beautiful as hell. And now she was his new next-door neighbor. He hopped off his front step and added, "I haven't had a chance to go to the store yet, and moving can really make a guy hungry."

She narrowed her stare, her forehead pulling down—no sign at all that she was as happy to see him as he was to see her. No realization that over the past few weeks he'd craved her smile, her touch, her goddamn *everything*. "How'd you get the lasagna then?" she challenged, her fingers pressing into the aluminum.

Yeah, apparently he hadn't thought that one through. He also hadn't thought out what to do if she refused to hear him out at all. He shrugged with a smile and stepped closer, taking the flicker of a second to soak her in. The way her long hair pulled into a braid that draped over her shoulder. The pinkie-thin straps of her shirt that drew taut against her tanned skin. The soft cords of her neck he remembered running his lips over. "Um…takeout?"

"Why didn't you get anything for yourself then?" No smile. No glint in her eyes. Shit, he needed to hurry and say what he wanted to say.

"Well…you   see"—another   step,   another   shrug—"takeout places down here don't serve more than one meal at a time to guys who are jerks."

Jerks. Jerks. Jerks. Yes, he wanted that word to penetrate and saw the exact moment it did. Her body angled toward him, and she tilted her head.

He took that sliver of a second to close the space between them, then he lifted the tin from her hands and set it on the small metal patio table beside the door. He'd thought about this moment for over two weeks—what he wanted to say and how he would say it. It was one thing that helped him through the move and the job searching and the downright acceptance that his brother didn't need his help anymore. Or…never at all, he'd come to realize.

"Melody," he said, resting his hands over her cheeks. Scorching hot. Smooth like marble. Damn, he missed the feel of her, the smell of her. "I was a jerk to you. A complete jerk. I never should have treated you like *any* of what happened to me was your fault. It wasn't. I know that. Regret it."

Her eyes searched his, probing, piercing into his very soul. Then her shoulders grew stiff. "You expected me to take—"

"A position at the hotel you had no interest in. I know. And I'm sorry." A smile tugged the corners of his mouth into his cheeks. "Did I mention I was a jerk?"

Melody chuckled, no feeling attached to it. "You might have to say it a few more times."

"Jerk, jerk, jerk…" Declan ran his index finger in a line from her temple down the side of her cheek and along her jaw. One minute movement, but weighted with everything else he wanted to do and say. And it seemed she understood that. Her eyes drifted closed in a slow blink, lips unhinged from their frown. In his eyes, it was the start to a victory.

"I can't believe you're standing here. Did you really move to California?"

He scrunched his nose. "Vegas was overrated. Besides"— he glanced from side to side—"I'm thinking a small town might be more my style."

She lifted an eyebrow, amusement glinting in her eyes. "Your style? I thought Mr. Vegas Performer would have liked a more bustling city. One with crowds and entertainment."

"There's a lot you don't know about me."

"Yeah?" She pursed her lips. "Like what?" A challenging

tone, though she looked far from angry now. More curious. Interested.

"Like my kitchen is stocked full and I spent the entire morning baking that lasagna and I have no idea how it's going to taste, but I just really, really wanted a reason to come over here and talk to you. And I think you look gorgeous and you smell amazing and I feel like I'm going to combust if you turn me away and tell me you never want to speak to me again, so please don't do that." The breeze gusted between their two townhomes, blowing a chunk of Melody's hair across her cheek. He brushed it back with his finger, securing it behind her ear.

A stain of pink drifted up her cheeks, highlighted even more by the sun casting down on them. "Are you really my new neighbor?" she asked in a weak exhale of breath.

He smiled, nodded. Crazy, he knew. But if there was one thing that could make him feel like his life was moving forward and not stuck on fixing his brother, Melody was it.

"What if"—her eyes zeroed in on his, question tipping her brows into a point—"I said I wanted nothing to do with you? Or that I had met someone else? It's kind of a big risk...moving here."

The curious tone of her voice was what gave it away—the fact that neither of those was true. He straddled his legs outside hers, pressing his body closer to hers. Leaning his face to her level, his mouth mere millimeters from hers, he said, "Not as big a risk as doing this." As softly as he could, he brushed his lips against hers. "Or this." To the side, he swept a kiss over one corner of her mouth, then the other.

She inhaled a shaky breath, her hands fidgeting at her sides, as if she wanted to touch him but was holding back.

He held her chin in his fingertips and tilted her face up to his. "Melody," he said, feeling like the words he'd been itching all week to say were about to burst out of him. "Please give me the chance to make it up to you, to show you I'm not the assho—" He shook his head. Shit, could he not say five sentences without using offensive language in front of her? "I mean…not nice person I was to you in Vegas. All I want is for us to go back to that very moment, right before everything fell apart." His thumb traced over her lips. "That moment when I realized there was something potent growing between us. That being with you took my mind off everything else and I was…happy."

His words faded out and silence surrounded them like an invisible bubble. The sounds of birds chirping and cars driving in the distance disappeared, replaced by only the beating of his heart deep in his ears. Seconds and more seconds passed, and just as he was about to step back, give her the space that her wrinkled brow was demanding, a gentle hand landed on his wrist. Fingertips closed around his skin.

"*Potent?*" she asked with a smile. Her fingers squeezed tighter. "Is that what you call this?"

"Intoxicating, powerful…they all sound corny, but other than 'freaking amazing,' I was drawing a blank."

She laughed, the sound like an angel singing in his ears. It washed over him like the warm water of a Jacuzzi.

"I like potent," she said, giggling, and his entire body tingled with the thought of spending more time with her.

"There's one more thing."

She traced a line down his arm with her fingertip. "What's that?"

"I'd like to continue your lessons. Three times a week.

For free."

She pursed her lips in a mock frown. "Only three times?"

He laughed. And then he kissed her. Hard and deep and with everything he had.

Chapter Ten

Melody shifted her feet, the rubber of her sandals scraping the short gray carpet of the airport terminal. Stale, cold air blasted against her skin, and she attempted to rub away the goose bumps rising on her arms.

One week. Declan had been gone only one week overseeing his brother's recovery, but to her it had felt like months. That funny twitch in her chest started up again—the one that always had her heart fluttering faster in anticipation of seeing her boyfriend.

Several people emerged from the long hallway that led from the baggage claim. A man and a woman. A family of four. Did they have a life-changing event back in Ireland, too? Or was coming to Southern California a vacation for them?

Black boots followed by tight black jeans and a rocker tee caught her attention. She'd only known Declan a month and a half, but she could recognize his well-built figure anywhere. Their eyes met, and he smiled, drawing another round of chills down her arms. Her feet itched to run, to close that space between them so she could throw her arms around him and feel his warmth. She'd gotten so used to being close to him—waking up with him, snuggling on the couch with him—that every cell in her body was anticipating that moment.

"Hi, gorgeous," he said, dropping his bag at his feet and scooping her up in his arms. He mashed his mouth against hers in a long but closed-mouthed, kiss. He smelled....like *him*, but also not the same. Did they use different soap in Ireland? She hoped someday she'd get to find out.

"Tell me everything," she pulled back and said. "How is he?"

Dark circles crested beneath his eyes, a reminder that his week in his hometown was not a vacation. Hospitals, doctors, and reconstructive nerve surgery were what filled his time there. And the exhaustion that came with caring for someone was ever present in even the way he stood, with his shoulders hanging forward.

"Doctors don't know if the surgery was successful yet. It'll take a while for the reconnected nerves to take, but he's in amazing hands."

"The hospital has the latest cutting-edge techniques," she said, repeating what he'd told her just before he'd left for Ireland. At her sides, she shook out her hands. "Surely they were able to restore function to at least some of the nerves."

He nodded then rested his forehead against hers with a weary smile. "Are you nervous, love?"

Love... Her mind tripped over that word and the memory of when he'd first called her that—just before he'd boarded the plane a week ago. Was that what she would call the flood of warmth that overcame her when she was near him? The ache in her chest when she'd lain in her bed alone this past week?

She breathed in the musky scent of him, calmed by the way it soothed her, and smiled back. "I just want everything to be okay. I want...*you* to be okay. And I know that won't happen until you've tried everything you can for your brother."

"The doctors there have a very successful track record with this type of surgery. He's going to be fine. I wouldn't have left him otherwise." He dropped a kiss on her nose then took her hand. "C'mon, let's get home."

The ride to their housing complex was short, and once they were at the split in the path that led to each of their doors, Declan followed her. Melody turned to him, noticing the listless way he stood with his bag hanging to his side. "You look like you need a nap."

He snatched the keys from her hand and nipped at her bottom lip. "I do, but I need to feel your body against mine more." He stepped around her and unlocked her door, swinging it wide with a swoop of his arm for her to enter. "Besides...I don't intend to sleep alone."

Inside she giggled. How many times had she fantasized about the moment he returned from his trip? *Too many— it's embarrassing.*

The bag thumped against the floor, and then his hand captured her waist as she passed by. He drew her in tight, his lips immediately finding her skin. He kissed her neck, her shoulder, every place that was bare and crying for his touch. The door shut, and then her back was pressed up against it, Declan's body pinning her to the wood. His hands cradled the sides of her face and a devilish grin drew up his lips.

"I'm not cutting into your work time, am I?"

Her fingers were already walking up under his T-shirt, searching for skin. "We'll call this my lunch break."

The responsibility of assistant editor had been daunting at first. So much she didn't know. So much to learn. But after a few weeks and the help of Karri, she was finally getting the hang of things.

Declan lifted her fingers and gently kissed each one. "Have you been practicing?"

She nodded. "Every night. I can almost play the whole song." Not as smoothly as he played or anything, but the chords to "Take Me to Church" were there and with even more practice, she knew it might actually sound like the true song someday. Had the intense practice sessions at the piano helped her reading? She couldn't be sure—it wasn't like music therapy was a miracle cure—but over the last month, reading through manuscripts had become a little less overwhelming. That had to be something, right?

Declan slid his hands into her hair, wrapping his long fingers around the back of her head. Holding her in place so he could run the tip of his tongue over her lips. The fire she always felt with his touch sparked to life. How had she gone a whole week without this?

"You'll have to show me," he whispered against her mouth then took her in a deep, lingering kiss. It was moments like these that she knew, no matter what her job, she'd made the right decision staying in California. Being with *him*. "Later," he added a minute later, pulling away just enough to say the word before lifting her off the ground and whisking her to the bedroom.

Acknowledgments

It takes a village to raise a book. This is my village:

Heather Howland, thank you for believing in my ability to write and choosing me to be a part of this fantastic continuity series. And thank you for an over-the-top gorgeous cover.

Alycia Tornetta, thank you for your patience, and for pushing me to be a better writer, and for being an all-around awesome person. I'm so lucky to have you as my editor.

Debbie, Katie, Jessica, Ellie, & Anita, a book wouldn't be where it is without an amazing publicity and marketing team. Thank you for being in my corner.

Robin Haseltine and KL Grady, thank you for keeping all of the authors in this series organized.

The rest of the Entangled team, you all work so hard. Thank you for your part in getting *Just One Reason* to where it is today.

My family (especially my husband, Ryan), thank you for

your support and for pulling me off the computer when the delirium sets in.

April Mann and Sarah Randolph, I couldn't ask for more supportive friends. I love you both. #girlcrush (Sorry, Sarah, I had to do it!)

Lisa, best sister and cheerleader ever. Love you to pieces.

My parents, thank you for never once doubting this journey of mine (at least to my face, ha-ha).

About the Author

Brooklyn Skye grew up in a small town where she quickly realized writing was an escape from small-town life. Really, she's just your average awkward girl who's obsessed with words. She writes young adult, new adult, and romance fiction. You can follow her on Twitter as @brooklyn__skye, Instagram as @brooklynskyewrites, or visit her website for updates, teasers, giveaways, and more. www.brooklyn-skye. com.

Discover the **What Happens in Vegas** *series...*

TEMPTING HER BEST FRIEND
a *What Happens in Vegas* novel by Gina L. Maxwell

Tired of waiting for her best friend to see her as more, Alyssa Miller heads to Las Vegas for a romance book convention. But when Dillon Alexander realizes his best friend plans to have a one-night stand on her vacation, he hauls ass after her to make sure he's the one to scratch her itch—commitment issues be damned. Neither of them expects their chemistry to be so explosive, but with a little help, what happens in Vegas might not stay in Vegas...

THE MAKEOVER MISTAKE

A CHANGE OF PLANS

MASQUERADING WITH THE CEO

TAMED BY THE OUTLAW

Also by Brooklyn Skye...

FRAGILE LINE